SILENT INTRUDER

Who'd break in and leave the house untouched?

When Michael and Hilda return from holiday to find two police officers awaiting them, a chaotic series of events ensues. The police have had an anonymous tip-off about child pornography being stored on Michael's computer. It's easy to prove his innocence, but who would do such a thing and why? At the same time it becomes clear that someone was living in the cottage while they were away, and may still be returning. Soon, they decide to take action of their own, with devastating consequences...

*Recent Titles by Gerald Hammond
from Severn House*

COLD IN THE HEADS
CRASH
DOWN THE GARDEN PATH
THE DIRTY DOLLAR
FINE TUNE
THE FINGERS OF ONE FOOT
FLAMESCAPE
GRAIL FOR SALE
HIT AND RUN
THE HITCH
INTO THE BLUE
KEEPER TURNED POACHER
LOVING MEMORY
ON THE WARPATH
THE OUTPOST
A RUNNING JUMP
SILENT INTRUDER
THE SNATCH
WAKING PARTNERS
WELL AND GOOD

SILENT INTRUDER

Gerald Hammond

Severn House Large Print

London & New York

This first large print edition published 2012
in Great Britain and the USA by
SEVERN HOUSE PUBLISHERS LTD of
9-15 High Street, Sutton, Surrey, SM1 1DF.
First world regular print edition published 2010 by
Severn House Publishers Ltd., London and New York.

British Library Cataloguing in Publication Data

Hammond, Gerald, 1926-
  Silent intruder.
  1. East Lothian (Scotland)--Fiction. 2. Detective and
  mystery stories. 3. Large type books.
  I. Title
  823.9'14-dc23

ISBN-13: 978-0-7278-9927-9

Severn House Publishers support The Forest Stewardship
Council [FSC], the leading international forest certification
organisation. All our titles that are printed on Greenpeace-
approved FSC-certified paper carry the FSC logo.

MIX
Paper from
responsible sources
FSC® C018575

Printed and bound in Great Britain by the
MPG Books Group, Bodmin, Cornwall.

ONE

In the basement below a luxurious house overlooking the upper Thames, its owner was relaxing. From outside, the house did not look luxurious; that was one of its many advantages. The garden was simple and slightly overgrown. The paintwork was peeling, the colours badly chosen. All in all it did not attract the interest of the tax inspector or other more common thieves. Inside was different. A professional decorator had been let loose with carte blanche but with a very definite brief – it must be both handsome and comfortable and, most importantly, it must look expensive.

Very few people got to see the inside of the basement, and those who did were usually sorry. It had been treated to as much luxury as the rest of the house. However his visitors might suffer, Paul Sweet saw no reason why he should suffer along with them. The deep-pile carpet was red for a very good reason. It did not show blood. Paul was a fat and sweaty man in his fifties, originally from Latvia (his original name had been Pol Zuis). He had made a name for himself among the London gangs. His modus operandi *was to plant one or more stoolpigeons in a rival gang and, when he knew enough and had the evidence to back it up, tip off the police who would then do his work for him. Just now, he was relaxing in the embrace of a comfortable armchair and enjoying a glass of brandy, a cigar and the spectacle of the naked man attached to the post in front of him.*

The post quite spoiled the décor but it had a definite function. It normally takes more than a single turn of rope to incapacitate a man, unless that rope is tied around the man and a post at elbow level and a crowbar is then pushed through and twisted.

Paul Sweet knew about the art and science of being a stoolpigeon so he'd had little difficulty sniffing out this one. He had considered planting him on a rival gang and then tipping off the gang, which would then have given him a worthwhile crime to hang on his rivals, but the man might have bought some relief by telling what little he knew.

David Cosby knew that his life was running out and none too soon. Breathing was becoming an intolerable effort and the sooner it could cease the better. Blood was seeping from a dozen puncture wounds and he had been worked over with a blowlamp. Death meant comfort and life no longer had anything to offer. Rose was dead. She had vanished and by the time he had managed to trace her it was too late; drugs and abuse had taken their toll. She had died in his arms but not before she had told him who was to blame and had passed on some titbits that she had overheard. David knew a policeman and approached him. The scraps of knowledge had been accepted greedily, as had his offer to enrol in Paul Sweet's gang. As a skilled forger, he was more than acceptable. Unfortunately he had been careless.

Paul Sweet stirred. The pleasure of watching the man's life drain agonizingly away had been satisfied and he had to accept that the few words Cosby admitted to having gleaned and passed on were all that had leaked, in which case the proposition was still alive. 'He don't know no more or he'd have told us,' he said. 'Take him away and lose him.'

His henchman, who was tall, thin, bald-

7

headed and very efficient, nodded. He knew what had to be done. He had done it many times in the past and no doubt would do it again. It was a job and somebody had to do it. But this one was going to be messy. He thought that he would probably delegate the work to somebody in the next level down in the hierarchy.

TWO

Michael McGinnis was born in Edinburgh to parents of New Zealand extraction. As soon as the business that they had founded together, wholesaling woollen goods, could provide for their retirement, his parents had returned to New Zealand. This coincided happily with Michael finishing at Fettes College with sufficient passes to admit him to university. He declined gratefully to accompany his parents back to the antipodes, and so they had left him in Auld Reekie, promising to finance him through university but no further. Mr McGinnis Senior believed firmly that to succeed in life it was necessary to start from nothing. With nothing to lose, he would say, you could afford to be rash.

Within a few years, Michael had embarked on a career in Information Technology. A friend had advised him that the activity would give access to all the fascinating subject matter in the universe, but shortly after graduating it had dawned on him that the subject matter coming his way professionally was usually boring and that the various professions allied to it were becoming overcrowded. While he was considering what his degree in IT might qualify him to undertake without too much tedium or effort and still enable him to keep himself and his girlfriend of the moment in reasonable comfort, a casual word in a local pub brought him into touch with a Member of the Scottish Parliament who wished to trace his own ancestry in the hope of scotching rumours that his family's estate had been purchased with money deriving from the slave trade. If he could produce evidence, however questionable, of a connection with Robert the Bruce or Bonny Prince Charlie, so much the better; but at the very least an industrial giant or a shipping magnate was required.

It had never been in Michael's nature to admit an inability to undertake anything short of childbirth. In searching out the required pedigree he had discovered that much of the information, which looked very impressive when presented in the form of a family tree with accompanying notes, was readily available on the Internet to anyone who knew where to look or by telephone from such sources as the parish clerk. Moreover, the profession of genealogist was not so crowded and, because the most certain route to money is to become very good at something totally useless (or at least with little or no practical application), it was remunerative. People were becoming more affluent and had higher aspirations. It also offered opportunities to tour around on his Suzuki motorbike, sourcing material and meeting interesting people, all before tax.

His first few clients were delighted and recommended him to others. The MSP in particular sang his praises. Michael had found that the family money had indeed stemmed from the slave trade but it had only been necessary to invent one marriage between his client's great-great-great-grandmother and the owner of a fleet of much more innocent ships and to fake sundry references to it for his client to be delighted. Michael discouraged the revelation of his real name or postal address, preferring clients not to see that he was working almost wholly without paper (his desk being cluttered only by his laptop, printer and a fax machine) but to imagine him surrounded by dusty box files and card indexes and perhaps several researchers bustling about to follow up every line that he could dream up. When he had advanced to the stage of advertising his services it was his email address that was used and few clients ever saw his face or knew his real name.

During the idle moments in his first year he had brought together the methods and sources of the work into a book of genealogy for beginners. When this was duly published, anonymously, under the title *Who The Hell Are You?*, Michael, with remarkable forethought, purchased at a remainder price the last 500 copies before it went out of print. Any enquirer who felt unable to afford his hourly rate was offered the chance to buy a copy at only slightly above the printed price so that he could attempt his own research; but the effort was strictly for the computer literate. Many of the purchasers became his clients.

Hilda Gilmour was born to well-to-do Scottish parents who lived in a prosperous town in Ayrshire. She could well have lived at home and found ladylike employment with one of the sound local firms. She found home claustrophobic, however, and sharing it with an overbearing sister with whom she was usually on the worst possible terms was too great a strain to be worth the extra comfort and security.

And so she moved to Edinburgh, living at first in a young ladies' hostel approved by her mother. She had taken and passed an advanced secretarial course. This had included much of the material covered in Michael's IT degree course but with emphasis on the practical rather than the theoretical. When Michael found that his business in genealogical research was being hampered by the need to slow down now and again to type with two fingers the essential letters and accounts and to deal with his filing, tax and VAT returns, he approached a secretarial agency.

Hilda was sent to get him back on the road, which she achieved very effectively, quite undaunted by a filing system modelled loosely on a municipal dump. She was much taken with the young man. His lean and academic appearance contrasted well with a definite hairiness. His blue chin and the traces of black hair finding its way out of the buttonholes of his shirt suggested an ample supply of testosterone and in this she was not disappointed. He spoke with a good accent and seemed to be making good money. Such things may not be quite as important as love, but love does tend to blossom when it sinks its roots into such fertile soil.

Her mother, who had been a raven-haired beauty, had prayed nightly that the early blondeness of her daughter would persist, but she was to be disappointed; the missing early pigmentation kicked in. Hilda became as dark-haired as her mother and just as attractive in that slightly chubby way, suggesting that while the owner might not be perfection to the eye she would delight the other senses. Those gentlemen who are said to prefer blondes prefer them slim; but those men are usually in search of a trophy. A brunette is more likely to attract a man who is seeking comfort and relaxation between the sheets, and for such purposes certain slight embonpoint is not only acceptable but often welcomed. She had a ready smile, a pretty face – even a touch of beauty when she allowed the smile to appear – and, so more than one admirer had alleged, the most provocative pair of legs ever seen off the screen.

Hilda owned a nearly new small car but Michael enjoyed the possession and use of his motorcycle, a masterly Japanese creation showing much chromium and polished stainless steel but still retaining the qualities of the British bike that had begat it and which was capable of speeds several times that which would be legal on public roads in Britain. He also kept a spare helmet for the benefit of female pillion passengers.

It happened that Hilda's car refused to start one afternoon when it was time to return to the hostel. Michael soon diagnosed a flat battery although her battery had been replaced only the previous month. 'Not to worry,' he said. 'I can put your battery on charge. I'll run you home and fetch you in the morning.'

Hilda looked at him while pretending to examine the spare helmet. He was quite attractive, well built, healthy and going somewhere. If this was a preliminary to an assault on her virtue her resistance might well prove to be only a token. But she was delivered to her hostel as intact as she would ever be.

Hilda's first trip on the pillion was a revelation to her. The sensation of speed was magnified by the openness and she was almost overwhelmed by the throb of the powerful engine between her knees and the knowledge that her safety, even her life, depended on the skill of the man to whose back she was clinging and whose muscles were shifting under her clasp. It was the perfect aphrodisiac but it was to be unrequited. At their destination there was a pause during which Michael considered moving in for a kiss but he decided that the risk of an angry reaction might imperil the order that she was imposing on his business. Each knew that something delicious was on the way. It may not be too surprising that two days later she accidentally left her lights on all day. There was another run on the motorbike but this time they turned east, away from Edinburgh and towards Norway. They found a long straight stretch of road, little used by traffic and never visited by mobile radar cameras, and there Michael demonstrated what the motorbike could do. All too soon the perfect road finished. Michael pulled onto the verge and twisted in the saddle. Hilda's eyes were half closed and her breathing had accelerated. He would have kissed her but the visors would have been in the way and he felt that in the time required for the removal of both helmets her enthusiasm might die. 'The hostel?' he asked. 'Or back to my house?'

'Your house,' she replied immediately.

The outward run had seemed too short. The return seemed to go on for ever but at last they pulled up at his door. Her knees were like rubber and his were shaking too. They left clothes scattered along the hall-way.

Michael was not inexperienced. He had learned over the course of half a dozen affairs always to be patient until the lady was ready for the next stage; but this time she was ready – more than ready. He had barely entered her before she reached orgasm. Instead of holding himself in check, for once he had to hurry. Afterwards, he got up from the bed and went to make tea. Next time they were more leisurely in their love-making.

She never returned to the hostel except to collect her property. It was the start of a very satisfactory relationship. They were in tune mentally. Moreover, being slightly taller than the average for a girl while Michael was slightly shorter than the conventional male ideal, when she wore heels they were similar in height. This, they found, was convenient both for dancing and for sex. Truly it was a relationship made in Heaven. Hilda's parents had their reservations but she was of age and could therefore make her own decisions.

After the first year, the subject of a holiday raised its head. They had worked hard; there was a little money in the bank and quite a sum due from satisfied clients. Autumn had arrived and the Scottish winter was approaching. There was enough work outstanding to keep them occupied during the

winter days when the weather would mili-
tate against outdoor activities. Now was
clearly the hour.

They each fancied becoming dog-owners.
A dog would enhance the country walks
that they enjoyed together and might encourage them to walk further as a valuable
antidote to a largely sedentary existence.
They had each admired a red setter that
lived on the same road and when they heard
that the bitch had been taken on a visit to a
stud dog it seemed that the moment had
come. A dog, however, would limit their
excursions on the motorbike. One holiday
together would fit the timescale. After that,
it would be a choice between the car with
dog or taking the bike and leaving the dog to
languish in kennels.

An additional incentive was that one of
their best clients had ancestors in Switzerland (although Michael would have favour-
ed Germany, where he knew that the speed
limits on most of the Autobahns were only
advisory). An exchange of emails with a
contact in Zurich would have produced all
the email addresses that could be needed to
satisfy the client, but a run through Italy

followed by a few days around the Swiss lakes would meet the same goal and would also be tax deductible. There was even a chance that the client, who was chairman of a toilet-paper conglomerate, could be persuaded to pay for the trip. The choice was not hard to make.

A few weeks later they were settling into a small but picturesque Swiss hotel. They had dined well. It might have been better if they had not enjoyed the imported Italian wine with dinner. After all, any occurrence, from the earth-shaking to the trivial, will have happened only because of a thousand happenings that went before. In this instance, if Mike had been quite sober, if Hilda had chosen to bring a different dress for dinnertime wear, if they had not dallied in Italy on the way, this story would have happened very differently – if at all.

Michael emerged from the terrace door of the hotel. The floodlights were not switched on. By the light of the moon and a remote lamp he saw a silhouette that seemed familiar and in a familiar dress, leaning on the balustrade and enjoying a view over the lake that included the reflections of moonlit clouds and snow-capped mountains. A late tour-boat was rippling the surface and broadcasting some rather dated dance-music. There was a scent in the air that he could not identify. It was a scene to stir the hormones of the most restrained man, and Michael had rarely even pretended to be restrained. He glanced around to see that they were unobserved. He and Hilda had arrived from Italy, where a pinch of the buttock may be considered no more than a well-merited compliment. Unfortunately Michael, in the mood of postprandial bon-homie, did not consider that a smooth but-tock was a satisfactory target, nor did he limit himself to the conventional pinch. On arrival and as soon as she was out of her motorcycling leathers, Hilda would have gone bare-legged. As his hand slid up the nylon, Michael realized that he had made a terrible mistake. He was about to say, 'So sorry ... Case of mistaken identity,' but while he was still forming the words and wondering in which language to utter them the lady span round and caught him a for-midable clout below the left eye. Her right hand was gripping a bunch of keys and it was a near miracle that saved him from losing the sight of one eye.

In recoiling, Michael caught his heel and fell, hitting his head on the balustrade – fortunately on one of the flat surfaces or he might easily have been killed. His ... what? Adversary? Assailant? Victim? The lady hurried into the hotel, throwing over her shoulder as she went some fiercely worded indictments of all molesters, stalkers, rapists and others who trouble the female sex. She spoke in English without knowing the nationality of the other party and was unaware that the addressee of her diatribe was too stunned to hear a single word. She also warned him not to follow her, which he had no desire to do and could not have done for a bet. To survive at all was, he felt, quite enough for the moment.

It was some minutes before Michael stirred and many more before he recovered his wits. He had the headache to end them all. He also had an urgent desire to be sick which he managed to indulge, leaning over the balustrade and anointing the bushes below. Luckily a pair of local lovers who were accustomed to making use of that spot had not yet arrived for their nightly indulgence. About the headache there was nothing immediate to be done. When the universe stopped rotating around him he headed for the bedroom, making much use of the support of walls and banisters. He met nobody.

In their room, Hilda was preparing to retire when Michael entered and rolled very carefully onto the bed. She could see at a glance that something was seriously wrong. 'What happened to you?' she asked. 'Have you been in the bar or did you fall downstairs?'

Michael knew by instinct that talking would send agonizing vibrations through his skull so he kept it short. 'You don't want to know,' he whispered.

It was against Hilda's most cherished habits to keep it short. 'Of course I want to know. If there's something wrong with you I may be able to help and if you're going to be ill I'll have to do something about getting us home. Anyway, I want to know what happened so that I can stop it happening again. I had a visitor while you were downstairs.

23

She was complaining that somebody assaulted her. That wasn't you, was it?'

'It wasn't like that.'

'What the hell is that supposed to mean?'

Michael realized that he had said either too much or too little. He forced himself to sit up. This made the room spin round but it was necessary. Like most Brits abroad he did not trust foreign water. He poured himself a glassful from the Evian bottle that the hotel proprietor had filled from the tap only that morning and drank gratefully. 'Aspirin,' he whispered. Hilda shook her head. 'Para...' The rest of the word evaded him but Hilda was quick on the uptake. She put two paracetamols into his hand and he drank again. 'Thought it was you,' he said.

Light dawned on Hilda. 'And you made your usual friendly approach?'

About to nod, Michael caught himself in time. 'Yes. She hit me. I fell. Hit my head.'

Hilda stood over him and parted his thick hair. 'I've warned you a thousand times to be careful about indulging in that little hobby. You're going to have a lump on the back of your head like half a tennis ball. Your left eye is going to close and it will serve you bloody well right. Estelle always did have a formidable punch. I should have warned you that my sister was the wrong person to tangle with.'

'Your—?'

'My sister. We do look rather alike from behind. And she was wearing a dress very like the one I brought with me, so I suppose the mistake was understandable, but you could have had the sense to be more careful. After all, I did tell you that she was coming.'

'You did?'

'Of course I did.' Hilda's voice took on the nannyish tone that always set his teeth on edge. 'I told you that she and Gordon – her husband, remember? – would be on holiday near here at about the same time so I gave her the name and phone number of this hotel so that she could stay in touch and know when we arrived. I didn't think she'd bother, we don't get on very well, but I did want her to meet you. She doesn't approve of our unsanctified relationship and I did rather hope that the charm that you manage to display when you think of it might win her round. At the least, I hoped that you might understand my point of view next time that she and I fell out. Unfortunately, I let it slip that her assailant was almost certainly my boyfriend. And now she's driven off breathing fire and slaughter. Don't you ever listen to what I tell you?'

This was too much. Michael forsook his vow of near-silence. 'Why would I? You never listen to me, outside of business. It's why we get on so well.'

Hilda let the point go. There was at least a modicum of truth in it. 'Despising me gives her a lot of pleasure. You've made somebody happy.'

'You suppose she'll be sure who touched her up?'

'She'll figure it out. She never misses a chance to think the worst of me, nor to say what she thinks.'

Michael, who had a younger brother and sister (both now in New Zealand), lay back. He was moved to speak. 'That's sad. I thought little birds in their nests were supposed to agree,' he said huskily.

'In your dreams! Some little birds push their weaker siblings out of the nest to die, so that they'll get a larger share of the food,' Hilda said.

'Did she push you out of the nest?'

'Not literally. But, figuratively, yes. I couldn't bear the place while she was still in it, bossing me about and throwing her weight around. By the time she got married and moved out I was in Edinburgh. I might have moved back home but you came along and threw me over your saddle-bow, whatever that is. The rest is history.'

'I don't remember doing a lot of throwing,' Michael said. He lay back on the pillows and tried to sleep.

THREE

Michael turned out to have a mild con-
cussion. There was a dull throbbing somewhere at the back of his brain, the idea of
food nauseated him and his vision was
double and slightly blurred. The symptoms
were mild and soon abated but Hilda was
adamant that she was not going pillion
behind him until she, not he, was quite
satisfied that he was seeing single and thinking and remembering clearly. They consulted the local doctor but he spoke not a word
of English, while their Italian was limited to
a few words gleaned from road signs and the
Internet. So Hilda applied her own strin-
gent tests. As a result they were three days
behind their planned return before they set
off for home. They made back a day before
they began the long run north, most of the
length of Britain. They had slept during the

journey through the Channel Tunnel and felt rested enough to ride through the night, aided by the empty roads, but they were still a day late when they skirted Edinburgh on the ring road and left it behind for the countryside of East Lothian. So far as either of them could remember, they had no important engagements for a day or two.

Michael's first employment as an IT consultant had been in London. He had found many things strange after an upbringing in Edinburgh and he had soon come to miss that corner of Scotland so, when he decided to become self-employed and that he would be happier away from the noise, smell, traffic, dirt and crime of a city, it was natural for him to head for the open countryside towards Haddington. The sale of his London flat enabled the purchase of a small house just outside an expanding village. Before reaching Haddington, they left the A-road for a B-road and a village street, left the B-road for an unclassified but surfaced road and, half a minute later, plunged through a belt of trees and arrived in mid-morning at a house made by a previous owner by throwing together two old cottages originally intended for farm labourers. The stone walls had been lovingly painted. Where once there would have been cottage gardens the house was surrounded by trees, although by judicious use of his chainsaw Michael had been admitting daylight and keeping his open fires supplied with logs. A start had been made to the restoration of the garden.

The house, of a single storey, was pleasantly proportioned although the roof line was broken by the incorporation of what had once been a small stable or byre with a lower roof. It was secluded. Even among the villagers, not many knew that it was there. When other locals were encountered and mention was made of Spring Cottage, most would nod and look wise without having the faintest idea where they would look for it. That day, after all the activity and scurry of their trip and the foreign voices usually raised in incomprehension, the two were looking forward to drawing its peace, privacy and developing garden around them like a comfort blanket, but as they approached they saw that the gate was standing wide and that a police car had squeezed between the encroaching bushes and stood outside the only door. There had been a frost while they were away and the trees were touched with autumn's glow. Two uniformed officers, one of them with a sergeant's stripes, were on the doorstep. They advanced as the motorbike made its approach, evidently expecting him to halt when confronted by the majesty of the law, but Michael rode between them and into the small lean-to that he had built for the bike.

The two dismounted stiffly, for they had been a long time in the saddles. The officers approached with the sergeant in the lead. 'What can we do for you, gentlemen?' Michael asked.

'How long have you been away from home until this moment?' asked the sergeant carefully.

'Just over three weeks,' Hilda said.

'You can prove this?'

'Absolutely,' she said. 'Let's go inside. It's cold out here.' The sergeant glanced around, surprised. He was no stranger to the cold.

'One moment,' Michael said. 'First tell me what you're after. Why should we need proof of anything?'

'We want to look at your computer.'

Michael thought for a few urgent seconds. There were few reasons that he could think of for such a request but he did not like any of them. 'You can look,' he said. 'But that's probably all until my solicitor's present. May I see your identification, please?'

Hilda made a small sound of protest but the sergeant only smiled. 'Very wise,' he said. The two officers produced their identification. The constable continued noting every word in his occurrence book.

Michael had toured Europe with just two keys on a single ring – the door key and that of the Suzuki. The ring was still in his hand. He unlocked the front door. The lock felt different. He wondered whether this was due to unfamiliarity or disuse but he decided not. 'Somebody had tried to pick this lock,' he said.

The sergeant made no comment but the constable wrote the words down in longhand.

Michael led the way into the sitting room. Ceilings were low and doorways were lower. The sergeant ducked as he entered. The place was cool but it did not have the cold and empty feel to be expected of a house that has been uninhabited for a while and has stopped pretending to be home. This was due to the electric heating being on at the minimal level for frost prevention. He and Hilda retained their leathers for the moment. They had left paper and kindling and a few logs in the grate and Michael touched a match to the paper. It was mid-morning but the room was rather dark. He left them for a minute while he turned on the electricity and then, out of habit, crossed to the table in the recently added bay window and switched on the charger to the laptop.

He found the sergeant at his elbow. 'You said that you could prove your absence until just now.'

Hilda had charge of all the receipts and credit card slips for tax purposes. She produced a fat nosegay of papers in a spring clip from her shoulder-bag, detached the top few and laid them in sequence beside the computer. 'Our tickets for the Channel Tunnel yesterday. The four credit card slips are for food and fuel as we came north yesterday afternoon and through the night.

33

I don't know what you're after but you'll see that the meals are all for two people.' She yawned, hugely. 'Can we hurry this up? We've been on the go for twenty-four hours and I'd like to get to my bed.'

'That may not be possible,' said the sergeant. 'Please sit down. May I see the other slips?' He glanced through the jumble of papers and left the room, which was becoming warmer and more cheerful as the electric heating added its help to the open fire. Michael removed his leathers and then sat. Hilda followed suit. They dozed. After some minutes the sergeant returned. 'I'm afraid you've had a small break-in,' he said. 'The bathroom window isn't latched and there are marks as though a small tool has been forced in. The culprit may also have tried to pick your front door lock, of course. You had better accompany us round and tell us what's missing.'

Michael had a question but he decided to save it for later. 'The few things that we have worth stealing, we had away with us – except for Hilda's car, which is still in the garage, and this computer. We'll look round later and tell you what's missing. First tell us what this is all about.'

The sergeant looked thoughtful. He had a serious face although the lines suggested that he smiled easily. He also had the beginning of a pot belly. Michael could imagine him telling police anecdotes in the pub.

'I see that you have separate credit cards,' the sergeant said at last. 'Subject to checking, it would seem that you were both abroad at the crucial time, so I may as well tell you that yesterday a complaint was received by email that you had been collecting child pornography on this computer. The complaint was anonymous but you'll understand that we have to follow these things up.'

Michael was tired but his brain came alive. 'I don't think that you can call an anonymous email a complaint. *Tip-off* would probably be the word. Or *allegation. Complaint* suggests that there's somebody there to complain.'

The sergeant accepted the correction impassively. 'A tip-off, if you prefer. It was received at about the time that you would have been boarding the Eurostar.' Michael made a move forward. 'No, don't touch the computer. Constable Murphy will open it up. Do you use any security codes or passwords?'

'Nothing like that. Everything on it is available on the Internet or other sources. Reports to clients are printed and then wiped off. We keep no record unless the client asks us to do so.'

Constable Murphy seated himself at the computer, lifted the lid and switched it on. While it was booting up he asked, 'Under what heading would any questionable material be filed, Sir?'

Michael had to laugh at the blatancy of the question. 'How the hell would I know?'

Murphy turned the computer so that only he could see the screen. They had to wait a few more seconds until it came alive. He was already wearing cotton gloves but he used the tip of a toothpick on the edge of the keys. 'Do you label any of your files PIX?' Murphy asked.

'No.'

Murphy keyed. He looked up, made a face, nodded and made a note in his occurrence book. 'Mild stuff but definitely over the legal borderline,' he told the sergeant.

Michael stood suddenly and took two paces to the side. The constable leaned sideways and the sergeant moved to block his path but he had seen enough. 'As you say, mild stuff,' he said, seating himself. 'I'm not the least interested in children. As for the people who want to make all photographs of children illegal, I can only think that they're deviants with sick minds to imagine that that sort of stuff can give anybody pleasure or that it would matter if it did. I can't see that anybody has been hurt.'

'That,' the sergeant said mildly, 'is not a matter for debate between ourselves. The facts remain that photographs of this nature have been proscribed by law. I am instructed to take action if these are found in your computer.' He nodded to the constable who made several notes and then set the machine to log off.

'I'll give you a receipt,' said the sergeant. 'I shall have to take away the computer. If your innocence is confirmed you'll get it back eventually with any illegal material erased.'

'Erase it now,' Michael said. 'That computer is essential to my business.'

Hilda touched his arm and gave him a headshake. 'Of course they have to take it away. We'll get it back. We can manage.'

'Very sensible,' the sergeant glanced at Hilda's left hand, 'Miss...?'

'Gilmour,' Hilda said.

'And you reside?'

'Here.'

Murphy closed the laptop and stood up. 'Just a minute,' Michael said. 'At least tell us when that material was fed into my computer.'

Murphy received a nod from the sergeant. He glanced at his notes. 'Yesterday morning, just before the email to us. No address of origin, probably fed in from a floppy or a memory stick.'

'All of it at a single visit?'

'I would be guessing if I answered that question.'

'We had planned to arrive home not long after that,' Michael said. 'If we'd stuck to our original plan we'd have found it much more difficult to prove our innocence. I take it that you'll be trying to trace the originator of the email to you?'

'Trying, yes,' said the sergeant, rising. 'An

38

offence – not the only one – has been committed, but no doubt we'll find that the email came from your laptop. Can you suggest the identity of anyone who has a grudge against you or reason to see you discredited?'

Michael turned to Hilda, intending to ask her sister's married name, but he intercepted a small frown and headshake. 'Certainly not,' he said. 'Everyone loves me.'

'We shall have to take your word for that,' said the sergeant. 'Now come round the house with me and tell me what's missing.'

The foursome trailed round the house, opening cupboards and drawers, until Michael was able to assure the policemen in all honesty that to his knowledge nothing was missing.

'And now,' said the sergeant, 'I must ask you to go away for a few hours. This isn't worth a team of SOCOs but at least I can get a forensics technician to take fingerprint and DNA samples. That won't tell us the culprit unless he has a criminal record – which may well prove to be the case – but it will provide proof if we ever lay hands on him. Give us until ten tonight.'

Under the close supervision of Constable Murphy, they gathered up clean linen and other supplies. They said where they would be for the next few hours and revealed the number of Michael's mobile phone. They had seen enough of the Suzuki for the moment. The battery in Hilda's car was too low to start the engine but to their surprise the two officers gave them a push start. The car soon brought them to a favourite hotel beyond the village. It was early for lunch but they ordered bar snacks and retired into a quiet corner with a beer apiece.

'You weren't very forthcoming with the cops,' Michael said. 'I can always tell when you're lying.'

Hilda flushed. 'No, you can't.'

'I can. You were lying when you said that nothing had been taken.'

'Nothing significant. I think somebody may have stayed a few nights there. Some food had gone and there was a faint smell of a perfume that I wouldn't even put on my bum. I didn't want to say anything until I was sure, because of the other thing.'

'Your sister, you think?'

Hilda gave a snort of derision. 'My sister,

I'm bloody sure. She always was a prude and she was fizzing mad when she left. And it's just the sort of sneaky, underhand trick she'd pull.'

'Yet you didn't say anything to the fuzz.'

'What good would it have done? It would be next to impossible to prove, and if she – or more probably Gordon, her husband, he's the computer-literate one – was convicted, what about it? She'd brazen it out and I'd be branded as the girl who threw her sister to the wolves. It would be much easier to prove the presence of that muck in your computer, and the damage to our business could have been fatal. It was sheer luck that we were late and the dates didn't fit the way she'd intended. We'll get our revenge, you'll see.'

'How?'

'If I knew how, I wouldn't wait. But if you wait, your chance always comes along.'

Michael yawned until his jaw cracked. They had been on the go for a long time. 'There was something else,' he said. 'Yes. I was going to object when they said that they were going to remove the computer but you made faces at me. For the moment we've

41

lost access to all our records and all the files of websites and...'

'We haven't, you know.' Hilda allowed herself a superior smile. 'I've got the whole lot on a memory stick hidden in a pair of stockings in the back of my knicker drawer. I've always thought you were a bit casual about the risk of losing it all in a fire or a computer crash or if the laptop was stolen, but you'd have got on your high horse if I'd said so. And we've needed a second laptop with the latest version of Windows, so that we can both work at the same time. This way we can claim it before tax.'

'I always said you were brilliant.'

'No you didn't.'

'Nor I did. But I'm saying it now.'

'Would you put it in writing?'

'No.'

When the waitress arrived with their food, she found them both fast asleep, leaning on each other and dribbling slightly. She thought that if that was what love did to you she'd stay single, thank you very much.

A few lunch customers trickled in. The ladies in the party thought that the couple looked rather sweet.

FOUR

After their overnight travel Michael and Hilda's sleeping pattern was hopelessly disrupted. They bedded early, slept like the dead and woke before dawn. It was fortunate for their long-term prospects as a couple that their reactions to such rockings of the conjugal boat were identical. During breakfast at a time when even the birds were only beginning to consider quitting their nests they discussed the next steps to be taken. Despite the certainty that the result would be a maddening interruption to their life and work, they decided that the police would have to be told of Hilda's suspicion – which by then was amounting to certainty – that the house had been occupied in their absence.

'You're certain that your sister couldn't be to blame?' Michael asked.

Hilda shook her head. 'Why would she stay one or more nights and risk being seen here? And Estelle would rather be raped by a mad donkey than pick up after herself. This person was a compulsive tidier.'

'Like you?'

'Yes, like me,' she admitted. Michael was just as compulsively untidy. (He worked on the assumption that the methodical way to be sure of finding things was to leave them where he had last used them. He then only had to remember the last occasion of their use to be reminded of where they were.) The result was a house in which compromise prevailed. Given a little help he could usually recover whatever had been tidied out of sight while Hilda had become reconciled to ignoring anything out of place until it had been causing clutter for at least half an hour.

By early that afternoon they were arguing desultorily over how to track down a police officer who they could count on to be uninterested to the point of telling them to go away and play in the pretty traffic when the sergeant from the previous day arrived, accompanied by the same constable.

44

Michael had already been into Edinburgh on the motorbike and done the round of the larger computer shops, looking for precisely the model of computer that they wanted and the shop prepared to give them the biggest discount and to pre-load, free of charge, an Internet connection and as many programmes as they deemed necessary. Hilda had discovered that removal by the police was not covered by their theft insurance and was recording the cost for tax deduction.

They were busily transferring the contents of the memory stick and checking their completeness, without breaking off a discussion that was becoming an argument, when the sergeant made his appearance. Hilda had a sudden fear that he had come to return the computer and spoil her little ploy, but his only reason for the visit was to explain that the other laptop would be required for evidence and might not be returned for some weeks, if ever. He even agreed to arrange for a letter to that effect for the benefit of the tax inspector. He said that there would be no charges arising from the material in it, except possibly against the person who had loaded it if that individual was ever identified.

The sergeant showed signs of surprise at being welcomed, led into the sitting room and presented with a cup of tea. He listened patiently to Hilda's suspicions and was then taken on a tour of the house.

'For one thing,' Hilda said as they entered the spare bedroom, 'you'd expect a whole lot of dust after being shut up for most of a month, but all the surfaces were spotless.'

'If the house was standing empty, there would be nobody to stir up the dust.'

Hilda shook her head in her most patronizing manner. 'There's always dust,' she said. 'Everybody knows that. And look how the bed's made. I do my corners the opposite way.'

'A left-handed intruder, you think?'

Hilda knew that she was being teased but she soldiered on. 'When we arrived home, it was bin day and the bin was out at the roadside. You were there, you must have seen it. But we couldn't have put it out for emptying and we'd left it empty. We always have to take it out to the roadside to be emptied and somebody knew that, so I'm sure in my mind that it was a person with a local connection.'

Hilda pointed out the gaps where some of her canned or frozen food had vanished and she drew attention to a dozen household objects that were no longer placed just as she would have left them, but it was clear that the sergeant thought this the result of an active imagination and a memory blurred by absence. He would, he said, make a report.

'That,' Michael said after the sergeant's departure, 'is quite satisfactory. He'll make his report, stating that he thinks you've gone bananas. Twenty to one it'll be filed and nothing whatever will happen and we can get on with our lives. If it ever turns out that we had an uninvited guest and that the police are concerned, we had reported the matter and then left it alone like good little citizens.'

'What do you mean, *if*?' Hilda retorted.

'I only meant if it turned out to be a matter of interest to the fuzz.'

As he himself remarked, nobody can be right all the time. On this occasion, Michael

47

was wrong. The sergeant returned two days later, but this time he was the junior member of a pair. He was accompanied and outranked by a Detective Chief Inspector Laird. The chief inspector, who was in plain clothes of indisputable quality, taste and expense, embellished by a few discreet touches of jewellery that Hilda recognized as being real, was a woman and a very attractive one. She was in her thirties but wearing well. Her hair, skin and figure were all cared for so that her cast of features was promoted from good-looking into real beauty. Michael let it be seen that, even so, he did not wish to be bothered with visitors. He had already been distracted from his researches into the antecedents of a new client, a racehorse trainer – with some Romany in his lineage, which opened up a new and interesting line of research. In addition, Mrs Gilbertson, a family friend, had passed on their trade name and email address and an email had just arrived from Hilda's sister, Estelle. He wanted to read it, think about it and possibly draft a reply.

This, it seemed, was acceptable to the visitors. Hilda was invited to lead them through her conclusions of two days earlier. The whole subject seemed rather small beer to merit the attention of a chief inspector and Hilda guessed that somebody even more senior had decided that a woman would be better able to judge the merit of those conclusions. This guess seemed to be justified. The DCI could quite appreciate how another woman might be familiar with her own idiosyncratic disposition of her various materials and implements and would notice immediately any departure from the usual.

The DCI was also wearing a subtle suggestion of a perfume that Hilda recognized as being very expensive. That scent jogged Hilda's memory. 'I've remembered something else,' she said. 'There was trace of a perfume still there in the bed in the spare room. I'm half sure that it was one I've come across before, though I can't place it. It was definitely not one of the pricier ones. Personally I wouldn't wear it for a bet. It's faded away by now.'

The DCI nodded, quite understanding. 'Would you recognize it if you smelled it again?'

'I think so. Yes, I'm sure I would.'

'If you do, give Sergeant Grant here a ring and tell him who was wearing it and where. But as soon as you start sniffing for it you'll probably find that it's as common as muck.'

'Probably,' Hilda agreed. Life, in her experience, was like that. They shared a smile.

'Do you know Mrs Greening?'

'I've met her once,' Hilda said. 'She was very helpful when I hurt my ankle. I slipped and fell near her front door.'

'If you should come across her again, try a sniff at her perfume. Let Sergeant Grant know anyway that you've seen her. She seems to have dropped out of sight.'

The two officers had arrived in convoy but in separate cars. The DCI drove off in a top-of-the-range Range Rover with all the optional extras that Hilda could imagine and an inconspicuous badge on the windscreen to say that the car had been subjected to modification and tuning by a specialist firm that Hilda, whose brother was a motor enthusiast, knew to be more than merely expensive.

The sergeant paused beside his humbler police Ford. Relieved of the presence of his superior, he was in a chatty mood. 'You know who that was?'

Michael had come out to join them on the gravel. He wanted to show Hilda the emails but first he was even more eager to be updated by Hilda. 'Who?' he said.

'That was Honeypot.' When his listeners still looked blank he explained. 'Legends about her are always circulating in the police. She was Honoria Potterton-Phipps until she married, so she'd probably have been nicknamed Honeypot even if she'd been as ugly as sin – which you'll have noticed she is definitely not. Her father owns a large part of Perthshire and is also an industrial tycoon. I'm told that the chairmen of banks take off their hats to him and step aside if they meet in the street. They say that she's the apple of his eye and he doesn't grudge his little girl anything. But you'd never know it from meeting her except that she has a car like I'll never afford, passed on to her by her dad. I believe the ashtrays were full. They say that she's brilliant as a police officer, that she didn't make her rank because of family connections but earned it.'

'I don't suppose she'll need to have her

family tree researched.' Hilda never missed the chance to promote a little business. Privately, she gave the DCI full marks for modesty. Despite the expensive couture she had not had the manner of one who believed that wealth excused all failings. 'Tell me, why the sudden interest in fetching senior detectives through from Edinburgh just because I think someone's been sleeping in my bed?'

The sergeant had taken a liking to Hilda and with the formal business over he was ready to let his hair down. 'You must be the Mummy Bear,' he said. 'Of course, you were away for weeks so you've been missing out on the rumours. I needn't give you the latest. No doubt most of it's all over the village by now.'

When the police Ford had carried him away, Michael said, 'Did you get the impression that he would be keeping an eye on Honeypot, ready to move in if her marriage showed signs of faltering? Come and see what I've drafted. After that I thought that we might have a pub lunch.'

'I was thinking along the same lines,' said Hilda.

After one or two minor improvements the reply was dispatched to Estelle, spelling out the terms and conditions of engagement. They kept the fees as low as was reasonable rather than scare off the potential client.

The village was an easy drive from Edinburgh so the expensive, upmarket hotel nearby that they had resorted to a few days earlier managed to sustain a good clientele of dinner and weekend guests despite the breathalyzer and the smoking ban, but in the village itself the locals were provided for in a smaller but just as well-kept pub. The hotel might cater to a better-heeled class of visitors, but the pub was where the latest and hottest news would be exchanged. The day was cool but sunny so they walked. Russet had not yet completed her inoculations but had already outgrown the puppyish habit of chewing and so could be left confined to the house. It was a sign that her puppyhood had been well managed, that she showed no signs of insecurity on being left. She was secure in the affection of her owners and knew that they would come back.

Successive landlords had removed partitions to throw together the several original smaller bars catering to different sections of society, so the business part of the pub now consisted of one long and rambling bar wandering round a central core where drinks were kept and food prepared. Those with higher social aspirations tended to drift to one end of the bar while those who either accepted or took defiant pride in a lower status settled in the other end. Because of the almost circular nature of the accommodation the two ends were nearly contiguous, segregated only by the doors from the entrance hall and toilets, but the arrangement was generally accepted. Local custom allowed customers to visit outwith their own areas but within the constraint of an unverbalized but well understood and practised system of body language.

On that day, a football match of local interest had attracted the dozen or so customers to the television set mounted between the doors. The usual conversation was limited to comments on the play or the occasional cheer or groan. One of the factors that had drawn the two together was a shared contempt for professional football. This was also shared by the licensee of the pub, a stout and jolly widow with unnaturally golden hair. Her name was Mrs Traynes. She was accustomed to make a joke of her name, such as that she had never missed a train in her life, but she preferred to answer to her first name of Matilda, shortened to Matty. After Matty was widowed there had been no objections to the licence being transferred to her name. She was a sweet person but a very tough landlady.

'I haven't seen you for a while,' Matty said when their lagers and hot pies had been served.

Michael opened his mouth to reply but Hilda got in first. 'We've been abroad,' she said. After that, of course, it was necessary to detail their route, describe the major topographical features and touch on local habits and customs. At last the conversation faltered and he was able to say casually, 'And what's been happening while we've been away? Not that much ever happens around here.'

Matty rose to the bait. 'There's been quite a lot happening this time, but nobody seems to know what. Strangers coming here for meals and listening to what's being said. The same men being seen talking to the local policemen. Questions being asked that don't seem to add up to anything much. Other men visiting Quimbles and being closeted with the big wheels; and nobody from Quimbles will say a word about it, even the ones who obviously don't know a thing. The word is that they've all been told to keep their mouths shut or else. And Quimbles is such a good employer that nobody wants to risk the sack.'

'Not even when they've had a few drinks?' Hilda asked.

'Not even then.'

Quimbles was the largest local employer. It had begun modestly as little more than a cottage industry but, being well run and employing the best and brightest minds, had grown rapidly. Products originating at Quimbles were now in demand throughout the computerized world, although not always under Quimbles' name.

Matty was called through to the far side of the bar. Watching so much energy being expended on the pitch had made the football fans hungry and thirsty. When she returned she said, 'Don't read anything into this, but the police seem to have been visiting Cairncross Cottage. Where Mr and Mrs Greening live.'

'Mr Greening is something important with Quimbles, isn't he?' Michael said. 'It sounds as though something funny has been going on at Quimbles. Insider trading or something.'

'I don't think it could be anything like that,' Matty said. 'Mr Greening isn't financial, he's technical. The financial staff doesn't come in here, they go to the hotel, but they say that Mr Greening's very good with computers and things.'

It was only a small diversion to walk home past Cairncross Cottage. It was in a street that was cluttered with parked cars even on a working day because the area was convenient for Quimbles staff and most of them walked in. But one car interested Michael more than the others. 'Policeman on observation duty,' he said when they had passed beyond earshot.

'How do you know?'

'Extra radio aerial, interior cluttered with

sandwich wrappers and empty soft drinks bottles, one man sitting in the passenger seat looking bored out of his mind.'

'I hope Muriel Greening isn't in any trouble,' Hilda said. 'She was very helpful last winter when I slipped on the snow. She took me in, dried me off and then took me to the cottage hospital to have my wrist X-rayed. She's a nice person. I liked her and I think she liked me. I meant to go back and call on her but I never seemed to have the time. I was thinking of inviting them for a meal, but now I'd better wait until this has blown over.'

'If she's "dropped out of sight" as Honeypot said, you'd have to wait anyway. But if you do see her, invite her first and then tell Honeypot afterwards. That could be our best way to find out what's going on.'

'Do we need to know what's going on?' Hilda asked in mild surprise.

'No, I don't think so. But it's always just as well to know the local news and gossip. Something's certainly going on and something more than a little bit odd has been happening around us. You know what happens to people who bury their heads in the sand.'

Hilda knew exactly what he meant but she saw no reason to pander to Michael's more vulgar streak. 'They suffocate,' she said, and changed the subject quickly.

FIVE

Life would slip back into its ordered rhythm soon enough but the arrival of Russet the red setter pup introduced a whole new dimension. Like any other pup, Russet was a bundle of fun and mischief, always demanding of games, walks and food. She was soon taught to mess out of doors, not to jump up and never to chew electric wires. As is every other puppy to its doting owners, she was perfection. At first she was brushed until she shone but common sense and moderation soon prevailed.

Michael and Hilda might have waited for years or for ever before their chance of revenge on Estelle came along. Or, of course, as Hilda pointed out, it might already have gone by or might have been passing unrecognized as she was speaking. Chance, as Hilda said more than once, always comes to he who waits, but it is not always recognized in time. However, it happened that shortly after the encounter with the police a family friend came to pay a passing call on Hilda on her way to visit a relative of her own in North Berwick. Mrs Gilbertson was a plump and jolly widow who lived near the Gilmour family home in Ayrshire and therefore near also to Hilda's sister and brother-in-law who had settled within walking distance of their parents. The early frosts had tinted the leaves to harmonize with Russet's coat but the day had turned into one of those perfect autumn days, dry and cool without being cold, so they took coffee under the spreading branches of a beech that gave shelter from the breeze but allowed the gentle sun to spread its warmth around them.

Mrs Gilbertson, who always enjoyed a good gossip, broke off in the middle of a soliloquy on the subject of all the changes and rumours in her neighbourhood. 'I'll tell your parents that you're happily established, shall I? And that you seem to be quite prosperous? Oh, and I know what else I meant to tell you. Estelle spoke to me the other day when I met her outside the library.' The lady's face and tone made it clear, if the fact had not been well known, that she had no liking for Hilda's sister. 'She's been trying to trace your family tree but even your parents can't get back past your grandparents.'

'They were very dull,' Hilda said, smiling. 'Nothing to record at all.'

'So she said. She asked me if I knew of a good genealogist. Of course, Hilda, I knew that the two of you don't get along – I can't blame you, frankly, but I try to be polite for your mother's sake. It never occurred to me at the time that she might want to engage you.'

'I've done some work on my ancestry,' Hilda said. 'It seems a pity to waste it. Not that it's very exciting. Shopkeepers and clerks, one mechanic and a small farmer. I'd be happy to do some more work on it if she cares to pay me.'

Michael spotted the opening immediately. 'There's not the least reason why you shouldn't give her our email address,' he put in. 'It's anonymous, so she needn't even know that it's us. We might just as well take her money as leave it for the next chancer.'

'Oh.' Mrs Gilbertson smiled conspiratorially. 'That seems reasonable. I shall enjoy thinking about her spending her money and not knowing that she's handing it over to you. Well, in that case, don't be surprised if you hear from her. She seemed very interested. I gather that some snooty friend of hers has just found Flora Macdonald somewhere in her pedigree and is carrying on as if it had been the Archangel Gabriel.'

'If we feel like doing her a favour,' Hilda said, 'which is unlikely, we might make her a present of Bonny Prince Charlie.'

'Or Rabbie Burns,' Michael said.

When Mrs Gilbertson had driven off, the two returned to the seat under the beech tree, but the autumn wind was freshening and chill. They moved indoors. Hilda made tea while Michael lit the fire. Russet immediately took over the hearthrug. There would be no shortage of logs: a large pine tree had blown down while they were away. They planned to replace it with a Canadian maple.

'I think you hit the nail on the head,' Michael said.

'Of course. Which one?'

'The one about Bonny Prince Charlie. If she does contact us...'

'She will, if she thinks that one of her posh friends is stealing a march on her.'

'If and when she does,' Michael said, 'we could throw in Burke and Hare.'

'The body snatchers and murderers?' Hilda's grin was enhanced by the firelight. She was dumbstruck by the beauty of the concept. She spluttered with laughter, spraying tea over Russet. When her voice had returned she said, 'I can just imagine her face!'

'I've never seen her face,' Michael said. 'Nor her bottom. I've felt it, though.'

'That's not exactly the thrill of a lifetime. And there's no need to be rude. We'll have to ask Mrs Gilbertson to get a photograph of her at the moment she opens our email.' Hilda paused and her grin widened. 'She'd do anything in the world to keep that piece of fiction away from her friends.' She moved onto the couch beside Michael and took possession of his hand.

Such inspirational moments have to be celebrated. Russet watched as they celebrated on the couch. She tried to join in the fun without quite understanding and had to be content with running off with an item of underwear which she later abandoned in the lane to the great amusement of the postman. Michael was amazed at the effect of having his bottom licked at the moment of orgasm.

SIX

Hilda looked up from brushing Russet. 'Let's email Estelle to say that we've found the Marquis de Sade among her ancestors,' she suggested. 'That should make her eyes pop.'

Michael admitted to himself that the idea had its attractions. His anger at the less beloved of the sisters was as hot as ever but the ploy would be seriously out of sequence. He rotated the typist's chair. 'You're not getting the idea,' he said patiently. 'We don't want to scare her off at this stage. So we tease her with – oh, I don't know – Florence Nightingale or Grace Darling. Once she's committed herself by boasting to her friends, then and only then do we begin to sow a few doubts. Give her a by-blow of somebody famous but disreputable.'

'Marlowe?' Hilda suggested.

'Yes, he'd do very nicely. Or Robert Burns. Then, when things are really humming, we bring in the transported sheep-rustlers, rape-victims, incest, you name it; and we tip off your friend Mrs Gilbertson to keep asking her in company how the researches are getting on. And I've had a real inspiration for when it comes to the crunch—'

He was interrupted by a hesitant rat-tat on the horseshoe door-knocker. Hilda, who had been sitting cross-legged on a cushion before the fire, jumped to her feet and went to the door, followed by the ever curious Russet. Michael could hear voices but was not interested enough to listen. They came back in a few seconds, Hilda looking puzzled. 'Do we know a man about my height, sandy hair going thin, a gap between his front teeth and rather a flat nose with enlarged pores?'

'It doesn't ring any immediate bells.'

Instead of settling down on her cushion again she took the second typist's chair beside Michael, who was ruling lines on a sheet of cartridge paper purchased that morning from the local stationer. The usual family tree or 'Record of Ancestors', excluding the original subject, runs to four generations and thirty individuals. Michael, however, wanted space to let his imagination run free and to go back enough generations to make any checking on his wilder flights extremely difficult. He was drawing up the framework to accommodate six generations and seventy-eight ancestors with space to extend even further when inspiration demanded.

'You have an evil mind,' she said lightly.

'Thank you.'

'My imagination may be running away with me...'

'Let it. But if it's a really wild idea, enter it in pencil and five or six generations back.'

'Not about my pedigree.' Hilda's forehead was creased by the effort of memory. 'That man who came to the door. He only said "Is she here?" and I said "Who?" and he thanked me, so that must have told him that she wasn't, if you see what I mean. He wasn't giving anything away because nobody's here. But the point is that there was a very faint perfume clinging to him, as though he'd been in the company of some woman or in contact with some of her cosmetics

68

and things. You know how keen my sense of smell has become since I stopped smoking?'

'I do indeed,' he replied. Hilda's heightened sense of smell had prevented Michael from following up a blatant invitation from an actress whose antecedents he had traced back as far as a notorious courtesan in Victorian Mayfair. Not that he would have succumbed to temptation, of course.

'Well,' Hilda said, 'I think it was the same perfume as I smelled on the sheets in the spare room.'

'Interesting!' Michael closed his eyes in the effort of memory. 'I met Frank Greening once at a party. It was only a fleeting introduction but I think he was one of several men who could answer to your description of our caller, give or take a bit.'

Hilda had gone back to the Internet, dipping into an invaluable Mormon website for the antecedents of a new client with a Texan GI grandfather. She looked up, frowning. 'But that would give us a neighbour, with a perfectly good home of her own – as far as we know – who spends a few nights here while we're away, and then her husband comes looking for her here. It doesn't make sense. I owe Mrs Greening a favour, like I told you, and I don't want to clipe on her.'

'But you did promise what's-her-name – Honeypot – that you'd let her know, through Sergeant Whatsit –' for a genealogist Michael's fallible memory for names was a disadvantage '– if you smelled that perfume again. It may not make sense to us at the moment but it may make sense to her.'

'Did I promise? She asked me to but I don't remember promising.'

'You promised. What's more, you don't know that your friend has done anything wrong. You might not be getting her into trouble at all. The police may be after her, wanting to take her into protective custody or to warn her that somebody is plotting against her.'

The screen flashed up a link with a famous Western outlaw. Hilda copied it to a reference file and returned her full attention to Michael. 'That may be perfectly true. I don't really commit to it but I was brought up to believe that the police only existed to protect me and other law-abiding citizens from muggers, swindlers and rapists. That may seem a naïve view today but it's a deeply ingrained way of thinking and once I abandon my nice, ordered philosophy and my trust in the infallibility of the British bobby I'll have to start judging every situation in its own light and on the assumption that the police may be wrong, which will be an unconscionable waste of time and mental energy. So I'd better give the good sergeant a ring. Pass the cordless.'

Michael tried and failed to reconcile the contradictions in that statement but he soon gave up and passed the telephone.

There was no immediate result of Hilda's phone call, but two days later DCI Laird appeared suddenly. They were walking Russet in open country under a picture-postcard sky, deep blue with a few small puffballs of cloud, and Hilda was throwing a ball for the pup when she realized that she was being observed. The DCI was watching her from the edge of a small grove of silver birches with such an expression of disapproval on her perfect features that Hilda came down off her cloud of contentment and felt guilty. She was not guilty of anything that she could think of but she quite expected to be taken into custody and Russet along with her. However, Honeypot's disapproval was not over police business.

The DCI had a shooting stick in her hand and two very handsome black Labradors tightly at heel. She was as usual smartly and appropriately clad, this time in a Barbour wax-proofed jacket, green Wellingtons and a headscarf. Any other woman might have been suspected of aping the Queen, but Honeypot looked so elegant and well suited that Hilda almost suspected the converse to be true. 'You are teaching that dog to run in,' she said severely. 'Telling it to fetch before or as you throw the ball can only lead to it dashing after the retrieve before the bird hits the ground. Always make your pup sit tight until a few seconds after the ball has landed.'

Hilda had been using the ball as a means of giving the pup a great deal of exercise without wasting a lot of her own time or energy. She had given no thought to Russet's adult lifestyle but she accepted that a pup of a gundog breed should be brought up to heed gundog traditions. Anyway, she was not going to quarrel with a senior police officer who seemed to know what she was talking about. She thanked the DCI politely. 'She hasn't had her inoculations yet,' she added.

DCI Laird called her dogs closer to her heel.

'I'll take her for a walk round the wood,' Michael said.

Honeypot thanked him. The Labradors sat like bookends. The DCI opened her shooting stick. 'Are you quite happy standing?' she asked.

'No problem,' Hilda said. She had been sitting for hours. She did not point out that she was at least ten years younger than the DCI.

The DCI seated herself. The breeze caught her hair. Any other woman would have looked untidy but on Honeypot the hair fell back into place. 'Now tell me again the story you told to Sergeant Grant,' she said.

Hilda repeated the story. The DI listened, nodded and then said, 'So no one person recognized both Mrs Greening and her supposed husband?'

'That's so. I recognized the perfume and I had met Mrs Greening when I had a fall in the snow. But I never knew Mr Greening. That was my...'

Hilda's memory for names made up for any deficiency on Michael's part, but on the other hand she was subject to sudden brief attacks of word-blindness. Suddenly, while she knew that Michael was not her husband, the word *lover* seemed unduly frivolous and the word *mistress* did not seem to have a male equivalent. As for *house-mate*...

Honeypot, now happily married for some years but possessed of a past of her own, recognized her disquiet and the reason for it. 'The customary term is *partner*,' she suggested. 'Confusing, I know, but that's the way that people mess with the language.'

'Thank you. I did know that but I went blank for a moment. So you'll have to show me a photograph of Mr Greening,' Hilda said. 'Or would you like me to get a look at the man?'

'Heavens no!' Honeypot looked and sounded shocked. 'Either would be quite improper. Identifications have to be carried out in a manner that will stand up in court. I have no idea whether there is any likelihood of that happening but one always has to assume that it might and I can imagine counsel tearing you into little pieces over that one if you were to admit that you had been shown a photograph or had the man pointed out to you. So will you please go and meet your partner and take charge of the puppy – who looks like growing into a very beautiful setter bitch, by the way – while I ask him a question or two.'

'No problem.' Hilda was much mollified by the compliment to Russet. There was little warmth in the autumn sunshine and she was glad of the chance to walk again. 'By the way, how did you find us here? You couldn't have seen us from near our house and nobody knew that we were coming this way.'

Honeypot smiled. 'You forget that I'm a detective. I'm also a police officer with dogs. The dog unit used to come under me and I still keep my dogs trained for tracking. I just allowed them to get the scent of your pup and this is where they led me.'

'As easy as that!' said Hilda.

'If you think it's easy,' said Honeypot, 'try it.'

'All she wanted,' Michael said as they walked homeward crunching on stubble, 'was to be sure of your identification. She had me describe Greening in detail that I wouldn't have believed I remembered. She has ways of making you remember things. His name's Frank, by the way.'

Their way home led them down the side of the stubble field and through a corner of a wood. They emerged into their own back garden, walked round the house and stopped dead.

'The front door's open,' Hilda whispered.

'I remember locking it.' Michael lifted from a stack of logs a limb about the dimensions of a man's forearm and weighed it in his hand. It was something that he kept handy in case he ever had need of a club. The village was only a few minutes' walk away, yet it could be a lonely place. He clumped heavily indoors rather than surprise an intruder. They toured the rooms but any visitor was gone; nor was there any trace of an unfamiliar perfume. 'Can't you smell anything?'

Hilda sniffed and paused. 'Somebody had smoked a cigar.' She added firewood to the embers in the fireplace and settled on the couch. 'You were going to change the lock. That old one must be easy to pick and the key is a monster to cart around. A Yale would be safer.'

'I don't want another key to be carried around and get lost. Yale-type keys wear your pockets and the bolt can be pushed back by something flexible unless you always remember to push the little snib back up. Tradition suggests that a credit card is the tool for the job, but it would have to be outdated or somebody else's credit card. I was waiting until we could afford a digital lock. Then you only have to remember a few numbers. I think it may be time that we raided the piggybank. We're beginning to gather possessions around us and we should either break the acquisitive habit or become more security conscious.'

'We spent the earth on our holiday,' Hilda said, 'but we're due several fees in the next week or two. We can spare a hundred or so. Why would somebody get in here, take nothing and go away again leaving the door open?'

Michael had come to a halt at the working table. 'Beats me, unless they wanted us to know that we'd been visited, as a sort of threat. And I'll tell you something else that makes less than no sense at all. While he, or possibly she, was here – and I'm assuming that it was the same person or persons – they added some names to your family tree. But I don't think that that could be what they broke in for. Come and look.'

Hilda, who had been enjoying a good sit-down after their walk, groaned, but Michael's voice held an intriguing note of puzzled amusement. She got to her feet. 'While you're up,' Michael said, 'pop another log on the fire. And switch the lights on; the daylight's fading.'

'That's the sort of opportunism that got you walloped by my sister,' Hilda said.

'But not nearly as much fun. Now that the bruises have faded I treasure it as a happy memory and you can tell her that I said it.'

'She'll treasure the remark.' Hilda put the lights on. The cosy room sprang into high definition and bright colour. She came back to the table. Russet, eternally curious, tried to push in front of her but was not yet tall enough to get her nose above the edge of the table. The large sheet of cartridge paper was filling up – with real names inked in the left portion while to the right the entries were in pencil. 'Mustapha P. Quiggley,' she read out aloud. It was several seconds before she recognized the indelicate pun. She snorted with laughter. 'We can't leave that in,' she said. 'Estelle would see through it in a minute.'

'No, of course we can't leave it in. Pity, though. It's quite clever. And there are several more in the same vein. They're in quite a different writing and I don't think there was any attempt to disguise it. Somebody wanted us to know that we'd been visited. But why?'

'To warn us away from making a fool of my sister?'

'I really can't see that,' Michael said, frowning. 'For one thing, nobody but our two selves knew that we're concocting a fictitious family tree. But to let us know that we're vulnerable so as to warn us away from something.'

'To warn us away from what? From giving a refuge to whoever squatted here while we were abroad?'

'That's possible, quite possible. Or just generally to wind our necks in. So, do we tell Honeypot?'

Hilda held up an admonitory finger. 'One thing Sergeant Grant told me is that she hates being called or referred to as Honeypot. She finds Honey acceptable. We should stick to it just in case she overhears us or in case we forget and use the name while talking to her. No, I don't think we tell her. For one thing, our preparation of a hoax family tree would be bound to come out and I'm quite sure that a lawyer could find something illegal about it. They could find something illegal about scratching your bum in a suggestive manner.'

It had not previously occurred to Michael that fooling somebody with a fake table of ancestors might be a crime in its own right even if not intended to defraud anybody, but now that Hilda had mentioned it... 'Avoiding all mention of that, we only have the fact that the door was standing open,' he said. 'They might well think that we'd forgotten to lock it. I think we'll keep this to ourselves for the moment. And now that the name's put the thought into my mind I'll have to go and pay a little call. For a pee,' he added when Hilda looked puzzled. 'Not the name Honey. The name Mustapha P. Quiggley.'

'Run along then,' Hilda said. 'I wouldn't want you to burst. Not in here.'

SEVEN

Michael rode the motorbike into Edinburgh next morning. The second ironmonger that he visited was able to sell him, at considerable expense, a digital lock of the mechanical variety – an electronic lock, he was told, would have been several times more expensive and much less reliable. He carried his toolbox out into the cool sunshine and was in the process of fitting the new lock to the old oak door when a shadow fell across his handiwork. He rose to his feet in haste. The newcomer had the look of a tough citizen and, although there was a mallet by his own hand, Michael felt vulnerable down on his knees and level with the other's kneecaps.

Despite a once-broken nose and scars over his cheekbones the newcomer, who was as tall as Michael but seemed at first glance to be several times as broad, managed to look like the better sort of horse with the same large, yellowed teeth. He had a mild and educated voice. He smiled, which made a feature of those teeth and yet added a veneer of charm to a face that had begun rugged even before suffering damage. His dark hair was cropped close.

He was also polite and well spoken. 'Would you be so kind,' he said, 'as to tell Mrs Greening that she has a visitor.'

Michael had no intention of being less than equally courteous to anyone as battle-scarred as this man. 'I would do so with pleasure,' he said, 'except that I have never even met Mrs Greening. If she is here, I am unaware of it.'

The smile slipped, exposing the rugged-ness beneath. 'Can you assure me, on your life, that she has never been here?'

The precise wording of the question, including the reference to his life, suggested to Michael that lying to this man might not be a good long-term proposition. 'As to that I have no personal knowledge. I just don't know.'

'You mean that you have no intention of telling me.'

'I mean that I don't know.' Made bold by the other's composure and impatient because the job was nearly finished and he was afraid of forgetting how to reassemble the lock, Michael added, 'Which bit of "I don't know" can't you understand?'

The man's expression did not change. 'Do you know who I am?' he asked.

'No.'

Without further comment or any warning the other drove a fist into Michael's solar plexus. The fist did not move more than a few inches but it drove the breath out of his lungs and paralyzed his breathing, putting him down on the path, wandering in and out of consciousness and rapidly suffocating. Life might never be the same again. Never before had he experienced hostility so physical and so violent.

The feeling of telling his lungs to pump air and having his orders ignored was strange to him. The world was turning grey but salted with flashes of coloured light that he knew were unreal. Life had become an eternity of searching for breath that would not come. When he recovered any use of his senses Hilda had rolled him over and was applying artificial respiration by mouth-to-mouth. Even second-hand air was delicious. The brush of those soft lips turned the experience into a strange mixture of pain and pleasure but pain predominated, mostly because there was a sharp stone under his shoulder-blade.

When pain and anguish rack the brow...

An hour later, Michael had been transferred to the couch where he was lying in state but with his head and shoulders propped up on Hilda's lap and a travelling rug wrapping his legs and torso. He was nursing a bowl of nourishing broth compounded from tinned soup with added ingredients from their embryo herb garden. Lying almost prone, it was difficult to take in soup without it running down his neck. He had by now recovered the powers of thought and husky speech. 'The bastard asked me if I knew who he was. That suggests that he might not have been so aggressive if I'd been in a position to tell the police who attacked me.'

Hilda was nodding. 'If you didn't know who he was there'd be less danger of you calling the cops – at least until the bruises had faded and the evidence had gone.'

She moved carefully, put a cushion under his head and got up. Michael closed his eyes and dozed, dreaming unfamiliar dreams. When Hilda returned, some minutes later, she inserted herself carefully under his head again. There was a ruminative silence. 'One thing occurred to me,' Hilda said at last.

'What?'

'I wondered how he or she knew when we were in or out. We usually know if we've got callers by the sound of vehicles and foot-steps, and Russet kicks up a din if it's some-body she doesn't know. Yet I have a hunch that we've been visited only when somebody knew that the house was empty. That was until your caller just now. But this time he wanted to ask whether Mrs Greening was here and see how I reacted, so he wanted to catch us at home. Perhaps you satisfied him.'

'You could be right. I have a feeling that he hit out, not because I hadn't told him what he wanted to know, but because I'd talked down to him.'

'Maybe. You do that a lot and sometimes it

makes me want to hit you. But I had a not very logical hunch that somebody knew our comings and goings. Perhaps he had come many times until he found the house either occupied or empty, whichever he happened to want at the time. Perhaps it was just the sensation of being watched. In terms of elementary physics there's no way you can feel somebody's eyes on you, is there?'

'No, but there are more things in heaven and earth, Horatio...' Michael stopped. The rest of the quotation had gone out of his mind.

'From the road you'd hardly know that this house was here, so I went out just now and had a look round underneath the trees where somebody might hide. In spite of the shade there's plenty of ground elder and ivy but I couldn't see any sign of anyone lurking there. Then I stood in front of the house and lifted my eyes unto the hills. Did you know that there's a peephole through the trees?'

There was a pause while Michael thought back. Hilda's fingers, which had been massaging the back of his neck, stilled. 'Not that I ever noticed,' he said at last.

'Well, there is. And it happens to line up

with a gap in the trees opposite, where the track to Piper's Farm comes out. It frames a large house somewhere around the far end of the village – an ugly brute of a place with fake half-timbering. The village lies at a lower level so that you can see over the roofs of the houses.'

Michael rolled to his feet. He found that he could stand without too much difficulty. He walked to the window. 'You're absolutely right,' he said. 'I wonder why I never saw it before. Of course, one tends not to look up, and if I was looking up I was looking *at* the trees, not through them.'

'If you say so. Can you manage to look after yourself if I go out for a few minutes?'

'I suppose so. Yes, of course I can.'

'I don't think the front door can be locked just yet, so be careful.' She left the house and he heard her small car drive off.

When he came to consider his state of being, Michael found that he had gone a long way towards recovery. His shotgun was stored with a helpful gunsmith but he decided that, if normal rules of behaviour were to be cast aside and violence was permissible, he had better bring his gun home and keep it handy. The law comes down hard on anyone who dares to defend himself, but better a period in the lockup than being at the mercy of any casual thug. Hilda's parting words were still in his ears. His thoughts went to his other weapon, the mallet that he had been using with a chisel while fitting the digital lock. His midriff still pained him and any use of his stomach muscles was a bad idea but he managed to make his way to the door. The job was so nearly finished that he went back into the house for a lightweight folding chair. Comfortably seated, he finished the assembly and was setting the combination when Hilda's car returned. She parked inconveniently close to the door. When her head emerged from the driver's window he said, 'Think of a five-digit number that we could both remember. No repeats.'

'If you'd move your chair I could get out and—'

'Number first, please.'

Hilda sighed, gave in and suggested a number that combined their birthday dates. This was put in and tested. Michael removed his tools and chair. Hilda quitted her car, carefully smuggling a long leather case so as to keep it out of view through the peephole in the trees. Michael followed, wondering. He disliked explaining himself or telling the same story twice so he was inclined to accept the same reserve on Hilda's part. The case was obviously heavy.

In the sitting room, Hilda explained. 'I called at McLeod's garage for petrol before we went on holiday. I got talking to Mrs McLeod while I was paying. She told me that her husband was getting interested in astronomy and he's got himself a telescope, although being downwind of Edinburgh the sky isn't often clear enough for a good view of the stars. I went round just now and borrowed it.' As she spoke she was setting up a tripod and mounting a telescope that extended to about the span of her arms. She was careful to keep it back from the window and in the shadows of the room. She looked through and adjusted the focus, then lifted the lower sash of the window a few centimetres.

When she stooped to the eyepiece again, she twitched. 'Golly! He looks so close that I was sure he could see and hear me. There's a sort of greenhouse on this side of the house and there's a man sitting in a cane chair. There's a table beside him and a drink and a big pair of binoculars and he's reading a copy of *The Scotsman*. One pane of the greenhouse is open and that's the one on a line between us and his head. He's definitely fat and nine-tenths bald. That wouldn't be your man, would it?'

'My man was in good shape with plenty of dark hair.'

'Just a minute.' She swivelled the telescope to and fro, slowly and delicately. 'Got him, or at least I suppose it's the same man. Long face, and even at this distance I can see the yellow on his teeth. Your man's in the garden, pruning roses. Not what you'd expect of a tough character but roses have to be pruned. Funny time of year though.'

'Not for ramblers. Talking of rambling, we might take a walk in that direction when I'm feeling a little stronger.'

'I suppose we might,' Hilda said doubtfully. 'Your attacker's at home and fully occupied so this might be a good time to take Mr McLeod's telescope back. I'll ask Mrs McLeod who owns that house.'

'Well, be careful,' Michael said. 'You know how word travels around in a village. The way things have been going it will probably belong to the McLeods. I do have a pair of binoculars you can use. I think they're in the hall cupboard. Nothing like that much magnification, of course, but they should do the job.'

It was an hour before Hilda returned, without the telescope but replete with information. 'That house is known as Mayview Lodge,' she said. 'I suppose because you can see the Isle of May. It belongs to the occupier, a man named Penicuik. Paul Penicuik. Mrs McLeod says that he's a bookmaker. He has several betting shops between here and Glasgow, but he has staff to look after them. He only turns out for the racecourse betting. She doesn't like him at all, I could tell by her voice.'

Michael had put mysteries and hard men out of his mind and felt recovered enough to sit at the table while he explored a new website that clarified the identities of French legionnaires, but Hilda saw that he was looking thoughtfully out of the window at

92

nothing. He took a few seconds to assimilate Hilda's news. 'That explains some of it,' was all he said.

She stood behind him and massaged the back of his neck again, just as he liked it. 'What does, and which bits?'

'I'm partly guessing because, as you know, I'm one of nature's non-gamblers. To me, the pain of losing outweighs the fun of winning and happens much more often, but I do know that you can't sue to recover a gambling debt. So it seems to me that the bookie only has a choice of two ways to go. Either it's cash up front until the punter's reliability is established; or else the bookie must have hard men ready to enforce payment of debts.'

'He could enforce a strict upper limit.'

'That would be limiting his profit. Ideally you'd want the client to lose all that he could afford and not a penny more, though if the punter loses more than he can pay I suppose that it hasn't cost the bookie anything.' Michael paused, frowning. 'Except that he's had money at risk, I suppose.'

Hilda spent a few seconds fiddling with the pencils that usually littered the table, for purposes of doodling or of making rough drafts. When she had them all in a tidy rectangle she said, 'That's a lot of supposition. Michael, I don't like the way this is going. I think it's time to tell Honey all about it.'

'If you're quite sure,' said Michael. 'But it may put a stop to our little game with your sister. Did she sign and return our conditions of engagement, by the way?'

'She did.'

'Then when we get around to publishing the details about Captain Goldbender, she wouldn't be able to stop us. Freedom to publish was one of the conditions.'

Hilda was beginning to grin. She craned her neck to see over the sheet of cartridge paper, which was beginning to fill up. Lines, it seemed, were going off in unexpected directions. 'Who in God's name is or was Captain Goldbender?'

'He was your great-great-great-great-grandfather. I think that's right but it's still subject to change. He was captain of a trading vessel that plied out of North Berwick. He took his lady friend – Wilma Darling her name is at the moment, although I don't know what she'll end up being called. Anyway, he took her along for what was intended to be a pleasure cruise to Bordeaux and back, but he picked up a profitable cargo to South America and he started trading on that side of the Atlantic and possibly round to the South Pacific, I haven't decided yet. It must be rather fun, being God. Anyway, it was some years before he got back to Britain. Long before that, he and Wilma had quarrelled and she took up with one of the crew and then another. All in all she produced four or five children and, because the captain already had a wife in Dunbar or somewhere, each was registered with the names of the next port of call for a surname.'

Hilda had broken down by this point in the tale, and was weeping with laughter. She blew her nose hastily and asked, 'What happened next?'

'They all returned here, of course, while the children were still very small. They were farmed out with friends or relatives of each reputed father and were soon quite unaware of their relationship; but these maritime communities tend to stay in touch and not to mix with farmers and others. So they met up and married, quite respectably—'

'But incestuously?'

'They didn't know it, but yes. That explains the sprinkling of the names of foreign harbours that turn up in your family tree and perhaps a few deformities or mental impairments as well.'

Hilda choked. It was some little time before she could speak. 'What breaks my heart,' she said at last, 'is that there's no way that I'll be able to see her face when she gets that part of our report.'

'We'll keep thinking about it. We might even invite her to come for a visit to heal the breach, or perhaps we could think of a way to video her at the crucial moment – that would be a clip to treasure. It would take careful timing. But, remember, the authorities are working hard to stamp out computer fraud. If there isn't a law against sending emails that don't come from the apparent source there soon will be.'

'I doubt it,' Hilda said. 'Anything like that would be much too sensible to come from any of our present legislators. If it did, we could find a way round it. One of my cousins is a lawyer and that's what lawyers are for.'

'Are you sure about that?'

'Well, it's one of the things they're for. That and getting the guilty off scot free.'

EIGHT

As they settled down to eat their usual light lunch, Hilda was thoughtful. 'I suppose Honey could wait a little longer,' she said.

'I'm sure she could. So what do we do?'

'We don't have to do anything. Something's happening but it's all happening of its own accord; we don't know what it is and I don't think we've had much effect on developments so far. But we could walk Russet in that direction and look at the house from outside, not too close.' She regarded him anxiously. He had refused to see a doctor. 'Will you be fit for a walk, after lunch?'

'I expect so,' Michael said. 'I'll tell you after lunch. But I'll also tell you this – he wouldn't have put me down so easily if I'd been expecting it. My stomach muscles were relaxed.' He set down his cutlery and looked at her. 'You know, you may be right, saying that we may not have had much effect on events so far, but who knows what effect we might have today on what's going to happen tomorrow?'

'That's always true,' Hilda said. She sounded surprised. 'But as to whether things in the long run would be better or worse for our interference, who could tell? On the whole, as you said or were probably going to say, it's the toss of a coin. So let's go and look at the house. We can let telepathy and our subconscious minds guide us to a decision by hunch.' She seemed perfectly happy with the logic of this *modus operandi* so Michael let it go by.

They set off an hour later, Michael finding that he could walk without more than minimal discomfort. What had once been the back door had been used as the doorway to an added-on extension housing a bathroom and separate toilet. (The previous minimal facilities had been merged with the new kitchen.) Rather than use the front door in full view of Mayview Lodge they left by way of the bedroom window, to Russet's delight. At Michael's insistence Hilda had changed her pale skirt for one in dark green. She was carrying a miniature digital camera. Michael had an equally midget pair of binoculars (a birthday present from his parents) and his only walking stick. The stick had been left behind by some previous occupant of the house, probably, he thought, as being too heavy to take away. It was thickly made of some heavy oriental hardwood, with an ebony handle that added to its weight. It was an unhandy aid to walking but its possession gave its bearer confidence despite its effect on his sense of balance.

Their most convenient route would have been through a back gate from their garden, but life is seldom so convenient. Except in very dry weather, the land beyond the gate was a bog. This was convenient when peat was wanted for the garden but except after those dry spells it was impassable without sinking over the ankles. There was also a small pool that held an unwelcome attraction for Russet. (As Hilda said, paraphrasing the Kwik-Fit commercial, 'You can't get wetter than a wet red setter.')

They circled behind the screen of trees and emerged through a gap in the hedge into the farm road. They followed the grass verge and after a brisk walk of five minutes they were entering the main street of the village. The first houses were comparatively recent, roughcast but already fading into the general pattern of gardens, climbing plants and slated roofs. Where the older, stone-walled houses began they entered a lane.

Russet could be let off her lead to stretch her long but still unsteady legs as they climbed a long slope between a field of wheat stubble and a sheltering tree-strip. The hilltop was broken ground, sprinkled with gorse and bracken and with sudden sandy hollows between. The bracken was beginning to die back, turning to the bronze of winter. This was becoming familiar dog-walking territory to them. Their usual path led away from the village into a tract of forestry owned, according to rumour, by a successful film actor for purposes of tax avoidance; but they picked their way along behind the crest until they thought that they might be behind Mayview Lodge. They looked over the brink. The miniature binoculars were powerful and in the bright day they gave a good image. The big house was below them and a little to their left. The man in the greenhouse seemed to be asleep but a dark figure was at work in the garden. A figure plodded in from the village. The man in the greenhouse roused himself, they exchanged a few words and the figure plodded away again while the man in the greenhouse settled down, apparently back to sleep. The mouth of the Forth estuary was spread out and the Isle of May crouched like a beached whale, almost central in its broad opening. The sound of insects was in the air. The whole scene was peaceful and somnolent, redolent of summer-becoming-autumn, but otherwise relatively meaningless.

From just below their position a dry-stone wall backed by a hedge ran diagonally down the fields to near a corner of the Mayview Lodge garden. 'So what kind of hunch do your telepathy and subconscious lead you to?' Michael asked.

Hilda produced a rueful smile. 'The distance is too great for the vibes to travel,' she said.

'Do you want to get closer?'

'I suppose we could look quite innocent,

just two people walking a dog across a field.'

'Except that we would be recognizable as us. But we could at least find out how far down the slope we could get behind the wall and hedge without exposing ourselves. And I don't mean *that* sort of exposing,' he added severely. Hilda was inclined to giggle at the least double meaning.

Russet went back on the lead. A red setter pup running loose would be certain betrayal of their identities. An expanse of gorse-dotted hillside lay between their position and the beginning of the garden wall. The gardener had his head down; the man in the greenhouse still appeared to be sleeping. 'If somebody seems to be looking this way,' Michael said, 'freeze. Anyone moving would be noticed, while a stationary figure at this distance would be overlooked. Walk slowly.'

They indeed walked slowly, to Russet's disgust. When they reached the wall, unobserved they thought, they found that a helpful depression, perhaps a former ditch, ran beside it. They were able to descend the hill without showing themselves for more than an occasional second or two, and those few moments out of concealment were also moments when a glance towards the house assured them that nobody was paying them any attention.

Their approach brought them to a corner of the Mayview Lodge garden wall which stood about chest high. The side wall of the garden continued ahead until it fetched up against the back gardens of the last houses of the village but, after turning the near corner, the back wall also ran away to their left. They squatted below the wall and conversed in murmurs. They could only see roofs of the village houses so it was reasonable to suppose that nobody could see them. 'I'm going to crawl along by the back wall,' Michael said. 'See what I can see or hear.'

'Be careful,' Hilda replied. She readied the little camera. Michael raised his thumb.

There was a gap between the hedge and the wall. The dry-stone wall had been butted against the well-built garden wall but not bonded to it and several stones had fallen or been pushed out by farm animals. Michael was able to crawl over without showing himself. A start had been made to ploughing. There was no helpful ditch and he was forced to move along a green strip between the wall and some ploughed ground in an undignified stoop, carrying his stick at the trail and with the fresh smell of the earth in his nostrils.

About halfway to a point opposite the corner of the house he was brought to a halt. There was a gateway that Michael guessed had been left for the purpose of bringing dung or machinery into the garden or visiting a compost heap that was sited just outside. Michael considered himself something of an expert on compost and this seemed rather an amateurish example with an excess of half-rotted grass mowings and no distinct shape. The gap in the wall was closed only by a gate of metal bars and he would have been only too conspicuous against the pale stubble if he had dared to go further. He tried lying prone and inching his way forward until he could peep between the lower bars but found that the gateway adjoined a vegetable garden. It seemed that the occupants of the house were not fanciers of rhubarb and so a rhubarb patch had been allowed to get completely out of hand.

He had moved into a crouch and was trying to peer over the taller leaves when he discovered that although his position might be less than ideal for observation, it was perfect for eavesdropping. The sound of voices and a peep between the topmost rhubarb leaves revealed that the sleeper had awoken and had joined Michael's assailant from earlier that day on a small terrace outside the greenhouse. Now that he was on his feet the former sleeper could be seen to be a small man but definitely stout. A drooping moustache failed to compensate for a lack of hair higher up but gave him the look of an angry otter.

'...Rain's not far away,' were the first words that Michael heard, in a surprisingly deep voice coming from so small a frame. 'So you're wasting your time at those weeds, Brian; they'll be as bad as ever by tomorrow.'

The man addressed as Brian shrugged. 'It's something to do while we're waiting. Anyway, I enjoy it. There's still no word of where the woman's holing up?'

'Not yet.'

'Give her up, Mr Penicuik. She could be in

Ireland or the Hebrides by now.'

Mr Penicuik chuckled. 'She'll have moved bloody fast, then, because she was buying food in Haddington last night. The punter who calls himself First Gasp recognized her. He phoned but Big Doris was slow off the mark and lost touch.'

'A pity. And there's no sign of movement at the other place?' Michael guessed that he was referring to Spring Cottage, the house that he shared with Hilda.

'Don't think so. I wasn't watching all the time.'

'There's probably no need. The way I belted him, he won't be walking for a while.'

Michael sneered silently. *We're not all little old ladies*, he thought.

'I don't think those two are hiding her anyway,' Mr Penicuik said. 'You were a bit hasty there, Brian. You may have drawn attention to where we didn't want it drawn.'

'Maybe. But next time I ask him a polite question, I bet he'll answer it. The woman's husband is back in their house and seems to be going about his daily business as if everything was as usual – except that he's having to do his own cooking and laundry. Alec

Jenkinson hasn't been in touch again?'

'Not yet. But he will. You can bet on it but I won't give you better odds than ten to four on in sticks of rhubarb. The rhubarb up front.'

'Huh! All right, I'll bet you ten sticks of rhubarb.'

Paul Penicuik chuckled. 'It's not your rhubarb to bet with, Brian, and don't you forget it,' he said.

'But I grew it and I like rhubarb, even if you don't. You're on.'

Michael's mind was busy with the implications of this banter and it was some seconds before he realized that it also implied an overdue visit to the rhubarb bed and the compost heap. He began to back away from the gateway but it was too late. The latch of the metal gate clicked. The man he knew as Brian came through with his hands full of rhubarb leaves and checked. 'What the hell are you doing here?' Brian demanded.

The last time that they had been in confrontation, Michael had got to his feet, but that had turned out to be a mistake. This time he remained sitting, with his stick across his knee. 'Walking the dog,' he said. 'And you shouldn't be pruning your roses at this time of year, except ramblers.'

A true enthusiast is easily distracted by his hobby. 'When should I prune them?'

'About mid-March, when they've started to bud.'

Brian nodded while slotting the information into a mental file. 'Don't give me that dog-walking crap. How did you know I was here?'

'I made a guess. Somebody seemed to know our comings and goings and this is the only house with a view of our front door.'

'How much did you hear?'

'Bugger all.'

It seemed to Michael that the other man's thinking led him, when denied information, to hand out violence on the assumption that this would ensure greater cooperation next time. He could see a return of the other's resolution but he had had time to think out his own moves. As Brian drew back his boot, his crotch gap widened. Michael used leverage over his knee to add force to his upward blow with the stick. He had only intended it as a warning shot – or at the most a tap to remind Brian that he was not confronting a helpless victim – but timing and angle combined to turn the gesture into a much more violent blow which landed precisely where it would do most harm. Brian froze, folding slowly forward. His jaw dropped open, revealing seriously uneven teeth, and his face, already leaning towards the comic, twisted into a caricature.

Michael was aghast – partly because of his reluctance to neuter a fellow male but more because of its probable effect on the dispute. In a book written by a former commando he had come across the words, *if a man has lost an eye he will fight all the harder to save the other one*. That, Michael supposed, was at least equally true of testicles. On the same page he had read, *if you must fight, fight to win quickly before you get damaged*. That seemed to be no more than common sense. He was reluctant to press the fight further but felt that he must. He climbed to his feet, suffering no more than a twinge from his battered stomach, and swung the heavy stick. It caught his target over the head with a crack that was either satisfactory or sickening, depending on the point of view. As Brian rolled his eyes up and went down, Michael saw that Hilda had been joined by an elderly gentleman with a Highland terrier on a lead. The gentleman was speaking into a mobile phone but Hilda held the camera up to her face.

Michael tried to smile for the lens but it was not a success.

NINE

DCI Laird – Honeypot, or Honey as she preferred to be known – looked across the table in the interview room without any great sign of pleasure. Michael returned the look and any pleasure that he got from it derived from her physical attractiveness and nothing else whatever. It had been made clear that he was not flavour of the month. The elderly gentleman's phone call had resulted in the regrettably quick appearance of an ambulance and the local police. Michael could only hope that if he had been the injured party they would have responded as promptly. As the apparent aggressor he had been removed to the local police station and kept there.

Michael gathered that the DCI had left a standing instruction that she was to be informed of any events involving the denizens of Mayview Lodge. It was his misfortune that she was concerned with other business at the time and it was several hours, during which time he had declined to answer a large number of questions, each framed on the assumption that he was guilty of more than had so far been discovered, before she made an appearance. He had then been allowed to explain himself – to a double tape-recorder, a video camera, a shorthand writer and Honey herself – in his own time and words.

Now it was Honey's turn. 'You've been lucky,' she said coldly. 'I hear that the man you struck – Brian Foley – is making a recovery. And we now have prints from your own camera. Your partner had the presence of mind to photograph the scene with your camera, in cine mode. Filming that way, she would not have had many frames available but, by good luck or brilliant judgement, she caught the beginning of the action and it is clear that it began while you were on the ground and he was aiming a kick at you. In those circumstances your response may have been excessive but I would not expect a prosecution to be successful. Whether he would succeed with a civil suit in the event of permanent impairment is not my concern. I am recommending no further action.'

Michael felt that this was no more than his due, but he was about to utter a word of thanks anyway when Honey stopped him with a traffic-halting gesture. (Michael recalled somebody telling him that she had begun her police career as a beat constable in the Met.) 'I am trying to convince myself,' she said, 'that you have not done too much damage – to my case, I mean, not to your unfortunate victim. As Mr Penicuik pointed out to his enforcer, the attack on you might well have drawn your attention to the place. But you will oblige me by staying away from Mayview Lodge and leaving the detecting to us.'

Michael nodded his assent but said nothing.

Honey went on, 'You are here as a witness but you have not told the whole story. You say that you suspected a connection between Mrs Greening and Mr Penicuik. Your approach to his house and what you overheard there goes towards confirming that suspicion. But what led you to suspect that connection?'

Michael looked away but there was neither comfort nor inspiration to be found in his surroundings. An attempt had been made to brighten the interview room with touches of colour and some artificial flowers but while this might come as a relief to victims, he thought that it served only to emphasize the severe look of the building. The green of the artificial foliage disappeared against the institutional green of the walls. The chairs seemed comfortable for the first few minutes and then quickly became excruciatingly painful. This, he thought, might have been intended to encourage a quick confession or denial. The room smelled of cleaning fluids and misery. 'My house had been visited several times,' he said at last. He felt that he was being dragged onto dangerous ground so he spoke with care. 'Once was a visit from Mr Foley when he offered me violence. I told you about that.'

'I referred it to the police surgeon, who examined you. He confirmed that you have bruising of the muscles over the diaphragm. Go on.'

'There were two other occasions.' Michael stood up. Nobody paid any attention – each had been relieving the back and thighs by means of a minute or two standing, now and again. 'One was when a woman took occupation of my house during our absence, but you knew about that. The other was a surreptitious visit a few days ago. You needn't ask me what he or they wanted because I haven't the faintest idea. The visits seemed to be timed according to whether we were at home or out. It was possible that abortive visits had been made on spec, but we noticed that there was only one house from which the approach to our front door could be seen, and that house, I found, belonged to the local bookie. The undergrowth beneath the trees around our house showed no signs of having been trodden down. Mrs Greening played the horses. The connection was tenuous but it seemed worth walking the dog in that direction to see whether my assailant was to be seen there.'

'You never told the police about that visit.'

'No. Nothing was taken. There was some slight disturbance, that's all.'

'If you tell me exactly what was disturbed

we might be able to guess what they were after.'

'It was a tiny act of vandalism,' Michael said. 'No more than that.'

'Tell me about it anyway.'

'It was nothing. Quite irrelevant to anything else.'

Not for the first time, DCI Laird ceased to be a charming woman asking for enlightenment as a favour. She happened to be standing at that moment, which made it easier for him to see, in her posture as well as in the tautening of her facial muscles, that she was a police officer first and that the beauty of her appearance and the charm of her manner were merely coincidental. Her voice became icy. 'It is not for you to decide what is relevant and what isn't. I am concerned with a larger matter than somebody visiting your residence, picturesque though it may be. Something is going on, we can't be sure what's happening or who is at the root of it. So far we have only picked up the ripples, far from the main disturbance, but we know that it is big. What has been happening here is one of those ripples. But if I investigate every ripple I shall piece it all together and know where they originate. The fact that Mrs Greening has disappeared may or may not be significant.'

'But I heard what's-his-name, the bookie, say—'

'From what you've told me so far,' Honey interrupted, 'if true and accurate, it would seem that your presence must have been detected at some stage. We don't know at what stage. It may be that the presence of an eavesdropper had already been noticed and that dust was being thrown in your eyes, for what reason I leave you to speculate. I therefore need to know all about that visit to your house – and when I say all, I mean *all*. Do you understand me?'

'I understand.' Michael said.

'Then spare me the need to remind you of the penalties that can follow attempts to mislead the police or to waste their time. How did you know that there had been a second intrusion?'

Looking back later, Michael could think of many perfectly good explanations that he could have offered, but at the time his mind resembled an uncooperative computer screen, stubbornly blank and promising to stay that way, while Honey represented authority and power. 'I did not want to reveal this,' he said, 'because I couldn't be sure what the attitude of the police might be. It happened that my partner's sister had served us a dirty turn...'

Honey, it was soon clear, was not going to be fobbed off with vagueness. She wanted chapter and verse and she was going to get them. Michael found himself dragged back as far as his encounter with Estelle in Switzerland. The only evasion that he managed was to downgrade his goosing of Hilda's sister to a mere pinch of the buttock. The false accusation of collecting kiddie porn was already on record.

When, aided by a few searching questions, Honey had the whole story, she said, 'Let me see if I've got this straight. You make your living by researching people's family trees. You had reason to believe that your sister-in-law, as we'll call her, had served you a seriously bad turn. Instead of handing the matter over to the proper authorities – the police – you decided to seek your own revenge. By chance you learned through a family friend that your sister-in-law was

119

being upstaged by a friend who claimed certain nobles and celebrities in her ancestry and so you coaxed that family friend into persuading her to approach your anonymous professional alter ego. You were preparing a family tree containing some fictitious and highly undesirable characters and relationships and, in order to keep your version straight and to forfend against contradicting yourself, you were working it out on a large paper grid. You knew that there had been an intruder because you found your front door open and that somebody had entered one or more extra fictitious names in the chart.'

'Four,' Michael said.

'And I suppose that these have since been deleted?' Honey said sadly. She looked at Michael as though he had been a puppy caught depositing faeces on the doorstep of Police HQ. 'Fingerprints and handwriting or even the names themselves might have told us something.'

Michael was surprised as well as pleased to find that for once he had done the right thing. 'As a matter of fact, no. I've been leaving them until the very last minute rather than destroy what might turn out to be evidence of something-or-other, if the entry into our house should prove to have any significance.'

Honey brightened. 'That's very helpful. I'll send a car for it while you phone your partner and assure her that you are being helpful and not in any trouble.'

They had time for an indifferent cup of coffee each, taken standing, before the chart arrived, carefully shrouded in clear polythene. 'The names in ink,' Michael explained, 'are genuine ancestors. Those in pencil are the first draft of fictitious characters that we intend to build into a story of crime, transportation, wholesale incest and every other vice that we can think of. Except for these four in the squarer handwriting.'

Honey had been keeping a straight face though Michael was sure that it was costing her a serious effort but at this point her reserve broke and she spluttered suddenly with laughter. 'Mustapha P. Quiggley,' she read out. 'Angus MacHinery. Arthur Itis and Ben Doon.' She laughed helplessly but in silence while dabbing her eyes with a fine handkerchief. 'Thank the Lord for one

121

laugh today,' she said at last. 'You don't know how I needed that. But I'd advise you not to be too obvious or she'll see through it and the point of the joke will be lost.'

'Our final report to her may not include many names ... The law doesn't disapprove, then?' Michael asked.

'This particular officer thinks that this is hilarious. After a day of being given the run-around, cursed for doing my job and obstructed at every turn, I was in dire need of a little light relief.'

'Thank God for that!' Michael could feel himself relaxing despite the nature of the chair that he was occupying. 'We were sure that there had to be some statute on the subject. There is one about everything else. Do you remember the song – the Beverley Sisters, was it? "If there's something you enjoy you can be certain that—"'

'"It's illegal, it's immoral or it makes you fat,"' Honey finished for him. 'There's a deep truth buried in there somewhere.' She paused and the light of amusement died out of her eyes. 'We might get the information we need by house-to-house enquiries, but at the risk of scaring the guilty parties, whoever they may be and whatever they may be guilty of, out of sight. For the moment, it's considered better to keep our enquiries confidential.'

'I'll speak to Hilda,' Michael said. 'We won't talk out of turn.'

Satisfied, Honey smiled again, but her eyes were fixed on his face. 'You can still speak to me. We had arrived at the same conclusion as Mr Penicuik – that Mrs Greening is still around but in hiding. Her husband is going about his daily business and refuses to say a word. This pattern has only been disturbed once. A constable recognized her in Haddington, probably at much the same time as Penicuik's agent, but lost sight of her. He reported by radio and another officer had their house under observation long before she could possibly have reached home. What you overheard makes it certain that she is not receiving hospitality from Paul Penicuik.

'The constable who saw her in Haddington reports that she looked clean and tidily dressed, so she must have access to facilities; or else she must meet her husband or a friend to be provided with clean linen. And, of course, she has to eat. Above all, she must have shelter. The local officer has only just transferred here, but you should know the area rather better. Can you think of any unoccupied space where she might have set up house?'

'There are caravans on Welch's Farm,' Michael said. 'Have you looked there?'

'Been there, done that, got the T-shirt,' Honey said less cheerfully.

'There's a disused pump-house down by the river but I can't believe that anybody could survive in it at this time of year. That's all I can think of offhand. I'm sorry.'

'Don't be. Before we part I'll give you a local map. In your comings and goings and particularly your dog-walking, mark on it any possible hideouts that you notice, but without drawing attention to your interest. And stay away from Mayview Lodge and all its occupants, please.'

Honeypot's last few words were innocent enough but there was something in her tone that sent a shiver up Michael's back. He soothed himself with the realization that he could now at least get away from those awful chairs.

TEN

Michael had a night of light sleep with periods of wakefulness. This was accounted for by his return home the previous evening to anxious greetings from Hilda and Russet, each in her own way conveying the message that he had been both missed and envisaged incarcerated or otherwise punished for his assault on Brian Foley. The thought that, but for Hilda's wise and competent use of the camera, he might well have been in serious trouble with the law and passing the night in a cell, kept intruding on his waking moments and into his feverish dreams. He could not imagine anyone else taking such swift and decisive action and he kept reminding himself that he must be nicer to her, even if that meant restraining the impatience that sometimes came over him at her tendency to treat him as a slightly imbecile four-year-old. That habit, he realized, stemmed from her relief at escaping from the domination of an elder sister and only patience and consideration would cure it.

He soothed himself to sleep at last by promising himself a long lie-in in the morning, followed by a late breakfast and an hour or two of pottering in the garden, so he was less than delighted to be dragged away from the breakfast table by the arrival of Honey, bent on his company in visiting Foley in hospital quickly, before his discharge returned him to the household and moral support of Paul Penicuik. Michael's compliant mood was assured by Hilda's discovery of two new clients among the overnight emails and by the arrival of the rain, which put an end to thoughts of gardening for the time being.

Hilda raised no objection to her lover being carried off by a very attractive chief inspector in a mint Range Rover with some very expensive add-ons, probably believing that he could barely afford even to buy that lady a pub lunch. Michael found that being a passenger, and in a higher seat than usual, gave him a better view of the countryside despite the rain, and he was able to point out one or two buildings in which he thought that Mrs Greening might conceivably have found shelter. Quimbles, in its own industrial estate, was up to capacity but there was in particular the premises of Cockahoop Ltd, a poultry processing plant that had been set up in some farm buildings just outside the town and which had grown and grown under pressure of business and legislation until the tail was definitely wagging the dog. The local authority would have been delighted to shift them into a new-build miles from anywhere but since the premises were still, by a small margin, agricultural they were outside local authority jurisdiction. By the nature of such buildings there might be leftover shed or roof space.

Hospitals do not welcome morning visitors before the morning's work is done, but the police have the right of way. Moreover, the management was waiting for the bed and a patient was already waiting on a trolley in the corridor. Brian Foley was found sitting up in bed, already washed and fed and with his clothes neatly folded on the bedside locker. A doctor had reluctantly pronounced him fit to go home but the constable standing guard had prevented him from getting dressed. Dressed in hospital pyjamas that appeared to have been handed down from somebody taller but thinner, Foley would have found a quick dash for freedom difficult.

Honey would have preferred to plunge immediately into her inquisition but Foley, far from resenting Michael, considered their exchanges of blows to form a perfectly satisfactory introduction with no hard feelings necessary on either side. Solicitous enquiries were answered with the information that Foley was doing well, that it hardly hurt at all any more and it was expected that he would be able to complete his uxorial duties when the time came.

An explanation of his friendly attitude was soon available. 'Hey! You saved my life,' Brian exclaimed.

'Did I?' Even Michael had difficulty viewing any of his actions in that reasonable light.

'You surely did. When they came to check whether you'd done me any serious damage, they found a lump on one of my balls. It was a cancer and they say that if it had been left even for a couple more months, my days would have been as good as numbered. They're arranging for an op in Edinburgh next week.'

'Glad to have been of service,' Michael replied, disarmed.

Honey sighed but accepted that more information was likely to arrive by way of friendly chat between two gardening enthusiasts than by a hostile interrogation.

'I never had a garden before,' Foley explained. 'Well, it's Mr Penicuik's garden really but he leaves it entirely to me. It's great, seeing things grow and knowing that I put them there. Like children, a bit, know what I mean?'

'I know exactly what you mean,' Michael said. 'When I bought my flat in Edinburgh the garden came with it. It was a small flat but a large garden. What I didn't really take in until too late was that the other tenants had access to it. They could sit in it or smell the flowers but I had to do all the work; and didn't they half complain if it looked untidy! But that turned out to be a blessing because one of them, too old to dig, was a retired gardener who enjoyed tidying it. He taught me a lot.'

Foley produced a broad grin, showing his uneven, yellow teeth. 'That's the sort of person I need. The neighbours know me for Mr Penicuik's collector and they steer well clear of me.'

'I'll help you any time I can,' Michael said.

'Well, what should I be pruning just now?'

'That depends. Some things only need pruning in alternate years...' About to launch into an explanatory lecture, Michael was brought up by a warning cough and headshake from Honeypot. He struggled to think of a smooth way to change the subject. 'But I'll run over it with you some time that Mr Penicuik isn't at home. Why won't the neighbours help you? Did you intimidate Mrs Greening?'

Honey sat back, satisfied.

'I never even seen Mrs Greening,' Brian Foley said defensively. 'Mr Penicuik said to find out where she was. He'd heard she'd been staying in your house while you was away.'

Michael could only think of one possible

explanation. 'Does she owe him money?'

Brian looked blank. 'I dare say that would probably be it. It usually is. And if that's what it's about it's probably a whole lot, because I heard him on the phone talking with Alec Jenkinson. But I haven't been told to put the frighteners on her and if I *was* told I probably wouldn't do it except in a very small way because I don't believe in roughing up women and Mr Penicuik knows it, but it hardly ever arises and he has an ex-lady-wrestler that he uses, so don't you run away with that idea. And that's all I'm saying. I don't want to lose my job.'

'Or your garden.'

'That's right.'

Michael raised an eyebrow at Honey and got a nod in return. Brian's tone of voice and body language made it clear that the time of confidences was over. Michael stood up. 'Leave the roses alone until spring,' he said, 'all but the ramblers. On them, cut back the stems that flowered this summer. The other stems will flower next year.'

'Glad you told me.' Brian treated him to another flash of yellow teeth. 'I was going to do it all wrong. Thanks. See you!'

Outside, the rain had stopped, leaving the world refreshed. A mild sun was trying to break through. As they re-entered the Range Rover he said, 'Foley's a strange sort of character. What do you make of him?'

'In my job I meet all sorts. What do you think?'

'I put him down as unintelligent but having had some education forced on him. Generally well meaning but, having been born with strength, he drifted into body-guarding or other strong-arm stuff. I don't think he'd kill but he'd be loyal to his employer, so given a conflict of interests I couldn't guess which way he'd jump.'

DCI Honey Laird seemed distrait. 'I dare say you're right,' she said absently.

Michael assumed that she was applying most of her mind to the matter of Mrs Greening and it occurred to him that a name had been mentioned that had not previously figured in the case. 'Who's Alec Jenkinson?' he asked.

It took her several seconds to bring her mind back. 'He's a big bookie in Glasgow. He has a stranglehold on the off-course betting market – smaller bookies lay off dodgy bets with him although you can't sue over a gambling debt. They know that he has ways of collecting – but he's also into fencing and drugs and vice and almost anything else illegal. And you didn't hear me saying that.'

'Saying what?'

'Good boy! Have you thought of Justin Case?'

Michael could not recall that name being mentioned. 'Who?'

'A name. For your girlfriend's sister's family tree. Think about it.'

While he thought about it, Michael was free to look around. He was usually the driver and, as on the outward trip, his viewpoint was now for once above hedge level. He was surprised to be reminded what an exceptionally attractive stretch of countryside he lived in. Mostly rather flat, it was nevertheless attractive and also fertile. He decided that he would not want to live anywhere else.

ELEVEN

Honey would have been pleased to know that such matters as intruders and missing neighbours were perforce suddenly relegated to the back burner. Hilda arrived at the breakfast table in the kitchen next morning looking subdued. 'I'm late,' she said. She sounded defiant.

Michael had been wondering how to break it to a Member of the Scottish Parliament that there was no trace of one of his great-grandmothers ever having married. He looked vaguely at her. 'Does it matter? We're not going anywhere. Or is somebody coming?'

Hilda gave him the look that she reserved for when he was being particularly obtuse. 'Do break the habit of a lifetime and try to think. Why would my being late for breakfast matter? I mean late-late. Really late.

Like days late.'

Gradually transferring his attention to Hilda's utterance, Michael tried several changes of emphasis and imaginary punctuation but the result was always the same. 'You mean you're really late? Days? Late-late?'

'That's what I just said. So I bought one of those kits from the shop yesterday. Then I left it overnight because I wasn't sure that I really wanted to know. Then this morning ... Michael, it says I'm pregnant. We were a little bit impetuous that time, a few weeks ago; we were a bit above ourselves just before we left for Italy. Things have changed. I'm not just one person now, I'm two. How does it grab you?'

The world had done a sudden flip while they spoke. Every parameter had changed. He was not a father yet but fatherhood was suddenly over the horizon. Michael had a literal and methodical turn of mind. 'We'll have to add another line to your family tree. How does it grab me? One, I'm delighted. I love both of you. Two, what will your parents think about it? Three, following on from that, might they feel that honour is satisfied if we were to announce our engagement before telling them about the little matter of a pregnancy? How does *that* grab *you*?'

When Hilda smiled it was usually a gentle glimpse of distant sunshine. On this occasion, however, she was incandescent. Every feature seemed to add its own glow to her face. Even her eyelashes seemed to smile. 'That will be something else to add to my family tree,' she said. 'I take that as a slightly oblique way of asking me to marry you and of course I will.'

'That's good.' For the first time since she had known him Michael looked shy. 'I'm not good at saying romantic things,' he said, 'but I've been looking forward to this. Having sex with you is superb; it's the pinnacle of my life, but I knew we were made for even more than that. I just didn't want either of us to feel committed until there was something to feel committed to. And now there is.'

She stooped and kissed him. 'My parents will be delighted and very relieved, but you were right. I'd like to tell them of my engagement as long as possible before mentioning any addition to the family. It will sound better that way. They try to be modern but they're still a bit old-fashioned. We should go for a visit. They should meet you, properly, and not just to nod disapprovingly to in passing. I'll phone Mum and make sure that Estelle won't be there.'

'That's the best idea of all,' Michael said.

Hilda's parents were enchanted by the news of her engagement. The news of her pregnancy was reserved for a much later occasion. Two days later they had tidied up their business correspondence and readied the house for being vacated for most of a weekend. Michael, who liked his own bed especially with Hilda in it, saw no need for a visit after Hilda had broken the news of the engagement over the phone, but he was overruled. On the Friday morning they locked up and left in Hilda's car. Russet travelled in her bed on the rear seat. She had done very little travelling by vehicle and they had been warned to have a supply of Sea-Legs with them, but they were relieved to find that she travelled well.

It was an easy day's travel, round the ring

road, along the motorway and south-west until the Firth of Clyde spread out before them. The weather and the countryside were constantly changing as they went westward. Although they stopped to buy an engagement ring from a wholesale jewellery dealer for whom Michael had traced an obscure but important grandfather, and twice to let Russet out for a comfort break, they had no need to hurry. In late afternoon, when each hill was casting its shadow on the next, they pulled into the driveway of a stiff Victorian house in a quiet street that was notable for the formality of the houses and the lushness of the gardens. Hilda sat for a moment, looking over the garden. She had forgotten the luxuriance that the Gulf Stream brought with it.

'Childhood memories?' Michael suggested. She nodded. 'Let's hope that our child has memories just as good,' he said.

'Better,' she said. 'A damn sight better than my memories of Estelle. If we have more than one – which is what I'd like – let's promise ourselves now that we won't allow any bullying.'

'That is a very definite promise. Was she

that bad?'

'She had the knack of hurting subtly without being noticed by anyone else.'

Michael decided to change the subject. 'I want a boy,' he said firmly. 'My father was seldom at home and I seem to have been surrounded by females all my life. Even Russet is female.'

'That can't be bad. We all love you.'

Hilda's parents appeared on the topmost of a short flight of steps and there was much handshaking and – after Hilda's ring had been seen, appreciated and admired – some exclamations and kissing. They were haled into the house – old fashioned, worn, comfortable and welcoming – and a half-forgotten bottle of champagne was unearthed from under the stairs.

Toasts were drunk, followed by muted conversation. 'We may as well eat first,' Hilda's mother said. Her father finished his glass of champagne and slipped out of the room and out of the house.

Hilda stiffened. 'Why "first"?'

'We'll have to tell people,' said her mother. 'They'll expect it. We'll have to phone round. Your father's gone out for more drinks and nibbles. All right, dear?'

'So far so good.' Hilda looked suspiciously at her mother. 'Who are you going to ask?'

Mrs Gilmour looked away. 'The usual neighbours,' she said. 'I'll jot down a list. Then you can phone them and that will let me get on with dinner. Invite them for eight.' She got to her feet. 'And don't forget Estelle.' She scurried towards the door.

Before her mother could escape the room Hilda snapped, 'Mother!' in a tone that stopped the older lady in her tracks. 'I was going to make it a day visit here,' Hilda said, 'but Michael said that it would look too hurried. I don't want Estelle to come. You can tell her any way you like but I don't want her at my engagement party; she'll just say something dreadful and spoil what should be my lovely day.'

'Nonsense,' Mrs Gilmour replied. 'It's high time that the two of you put aside these childish squabbles. If you behave nicely I'm sure Estelle will do the same. Anyway, I'll tell her that there's to be no backbiting.'

Hilda managed to refrain from the tantrum that this exchange would have provoked a few years earlier. 'There you are!' she exclaimed. 'You wouldn't have said that if you hadn't known that Estelle always starts trouble. Do you honestly think that a word from you will change the habit of years?'

Mrs Gilmour drew herself up and Hilda knew, with a sinking feeling of certainty, that her mother was resuming the mantle of materfamilias. 'Hilda, whatever the facts of the matter, you know as well as I do that if we don't invite her along you'll be gone and your father and I will be left to bear the brunt of endless complaints and arguments and she'll be going round everybody inventing horrible reasons for our being so secretive.'

Hilda heaved a sigh that nearly fluttered the curtains. She felt empowered by her new status as a soon-to-be-married and independent woman to speak frankly as never before. 'That is a more credible argument. All right then, Mother, now that you recognize the problem at long last, I'll accept Estelle for your sake only. But read the riot act and fire over her head or Michael and I will get straight into my car and go home, and then what will the neighbours think? And I mean that seriously.'

* * *

In the event, the party turned out well. There was a crowd of neighbours, all in sentimental mood. Some brought bottles. The big sitting room became stuffier, the voices louder. Estelle wished her sister good luck with, as far as anyone could see, every sign of sincerity. Questions as to when they intended to tie the knot were parried with the evasion 'soon', and the enquirers could make of that whatever they would. Russet was a great favourite and developed a strong attachment to Mrs Gilbertson, who treated her to surreptitious crisps. She soon learned to open the packet for herself.

After consultation with her daughter and not without some hidden reservations, Mrs Gilmour had permitted that the young couple should share what had once been Hilda's bedroom. As they prepared for bed, Hilda, still in party mood, said, 'My sister seems to have turned over a new leaf. I'm tempted to suggest we abandon the dirty tricks after all. It's a shame to waste all that inventive thinking but perhaps it's time that we looked for peace within the family.'

The sight of Hilda emerging from her

pretty clothes had not yet staled for Michael but this comment was enough to fetch him back slowly into current reality. 'Do you really mean it?' he asked.

Hilda, exquisite in silk bra and pants, shrugged. 'I don't know. I had a chat with her and I worked carefully around to the fact that we'd been subjected to a false allegation. She acted very surprised and when I said that I thought that somebody had been in our house while we were abroad she said that surely I was mistaken. She was very convincing, but then she always had that knack. Until I learned better, she could look me in the eye and tell me that black was—'

She had finished disrobing and Michael had another thing on his mind. He swept her off her feet. She pretended to struggle. They moved gently to avoid calling attention to the squeaking of bedsprings and for the sake of the foetus who was becoming a real person to them. It was a most successful and fulfilling coupling.

When passion was spent at last Michael said, 'All right, if that's what you really and truly want. Little birds in their nest should agree, though some might say that it's a little late now to be starting afresh. I'm not altogether confident that your mother's words to Estelle have really borne fruit. She behaved very well in front of your neighbours, but when she wished me luck she added, "You'll need it".'

Hilda's nostrils flared. Michael could imagine steam or even smoke coming from them. 'She said that, did she?' Hilda ground out. 'Then go ahead and think up the very worst, the most immoral, dishonest, corrupt, diseased, debt-ridden character that you can possibly envisage and then I'll add a few touches of my own and we'll include him. Or her,' Hilda added fairly. 'I think it should be somebody altogether fictitious. That way we can let our imaginations have free rein.'

They settled down to a repose interrupted only by whispered discussion and occasional little snorts of laughter.

Hilda's father, who was financial director to a medium-sized firm of wholesalers, had a meeting next morning and Mrs Gilmour, refusing offers of help, wanted a little time with her home help to clear up the previous

144

evening's debris and to prepare meals for the remainder of the weekend. Hilda and Michael were free for the morning.

They dawdled around the shops and made some minor purchases for the house and garden. On their way back to the Gilmour house with an hour in hand, they called at the largest local hotel. On a Saturday and shortly before lunchtime, the cocktail bar was at least half full but they found a table to themselves in a bay window and watched the passers-by. The leaves were still clinging to the trees but the flowers were over.

'Do you feel like a stranger?' Michael asked.

'Not yet. I haven't been away for long and nothing changes quickly here. Not even Estelle.'

'Last night you were suggesting that we might abandon the trick family tree.'

'You had put me in a mood of tender acceptance.'

'I'm delighted that I have that effect. So much was going on last night and so much wine had flowed that I wasn't taking half of it in. Thinking back, she wished me luck. Then she whispered something that sounded like, "You'll need it". I told you that, didn't I?'

'You did. And that's when I changed my mind and said that we would hit her where it hurt. Damn!' She leaned back from the glass. 'There goes Estelle now, on the way home from church. I hope she didn't see me.'

It was soon clear that Hilda's hope was in vain. Estelle entered the cocktail bar and headed in their direction, followed by her husband. Gordon Bute was a tall, slightly gangling figure with cropped, reddish hair, neat beard and whiskers and an evident fear of his wife. His most noticeable feature was a large wristwatch, very macho, covered in knobs and dials few of which he had ever come to understand. He had not been present at the previous evening's festivities. Several confused minutes passed in introductions, the moving of chairs and Gordon being sent for a round of drinks. Estelle's manner was difficult to read. She made it clear that the little matter of fingers up her behind and her violent reply were forgiven and, as far as she was concerned, forgotten or at least put aside for the moment.

Michael thought that there might be trouble in the offing.

When they were settled, Gordon proffered his congratulations. 'When do you plan to tie the knot?' he asked.

'Soon,' Hilda said. 'Why wait? I'm not looking for something fancy and expensive.'

Estelle bridled. 'Like mine, you mean?'

Hilda made one more attempt to avoid open friction. 'I didn't say that and I wasn't thinking it.'

'Of course not,' said Gordon. 'I seem to remember that the moving spirit was your mother, Hilda. She said, quite openly, that she didn't want the townsfolk saying that they couldn't push the boat out for their first daughter.'

'She'll say the same again,' Estelle prophesied. 'Except that you're not the first. Will you go along with it? Or...' Her eyes narrowed. 'Are you pregnant? Is that the reason for the hurry? And for not wanting a big white wedding?'

'Somebody said that a wedding was just a ghastly public declaration of a strictly private intention, or words to that effect. Probably Oscar.'

Estelle was not going to allow her to evade the subject. 'Are you pregnant?' she asked again.

Hilda's chin came up. 'If I was, it would be no business of yours.'

Estelle matched her, look for look. 'It would, you know. This has always been a respectable family. There's never been the faintest hint of scandal.'

'That you know of,' said Hilda.

'I'm sure of it. I hope you're not going to be the one to put the bar sinister onto our crest.'

Hilda and Michael exchanged eye contact and faint nods. 'I think Hilda told you,' said Michael, 'that we had at least one intruder during our absence. We called the police, of course. They collected fingerprints and DNA.'

'Meaning?'

'Meaning that they're taking it very seriously. It seems to be part and parcel of something bigger, so they were asking for the names and addresses of all our friends and relatives. I'm telling you this so that you won't be too surprised if the police come around looking for samples.'

'It would have looked very suspicious if we'd left your name off the list,' added Hilda.

Gordon was nodding. 'Of course it would,' he said. Estelle skewered him with a venomous glare.

Michael leaned forward. 'Are you sure that you didn't see anybody at our house?' he asked.

Estelle shook her head. 'Nobody,' she said. Then she jumped and spilled a few drops of her gin and tonic. 'I've never been to your house.'

Michael leaned back and smiled. 'Of course. I'd forgotten. We'll have to have you through some time.'

'In a few years,' Hilda said. 'But not too few.'

Estelle bit her lip. 'You keep some funny company,' she ground out. She finished her drink and dragged her husband away much more quickly than was polite, before she could be asked any questions about how she knew what sort of company they kept.

'That settles it,' Hilda said. 'Let's go for the jugular.'

'And the jugular the better,' Michael said.

'How did two such people as your parents, both polite and kind, manage to produce that harpy and then ... Well, when I worry about how you're going to turn out, later in life, I try to think of your mother and not Estelle.'

TWELVE

They left for home on the Sunday morning, their ears ringing with good wishes, wedding plans and advice to the lovelorn. In the car, they rediscovered their sense of being a private and isolated couple. They were in their own little bubble where they were safe from being overheard and from the sudden appearance of anxious relatives.

'She'd been in our house, right enough,' Hilda said suddenly.

'That's what I was just thinking. She was torn between refusing to admit it and being desperate to confront us with something that she'd seen.'

'Somebody told me that couples who live and work together often develop telepathy. Is that happening to us?'

Michael was taking a turn at the driving. He waited until he was clear of a lumbering tractor and trailer before replying. 'I think so. Is that your way of saying that you had been reading your sister the same way?'

'Exactly. And, at that time, the only thing she could have seen that would have had any significance for her, unless she only wanted to needle us about the slightly second-hand look of the place, would have been a person, which would explain her remark about the company we keep.'

'Mrs Greening?'

'I think so. Muriel Greening's a lovely person, heart of gold and all that jazz, but she's not exactly out of the top drawer and Estelle's the snob of all snobs. That would have been when we were later getting back from our trip than she was expecting.'

They were on the Edinburgh motorway and Hilda was driving before she said, 'Could Muriel Greening still be using our house?'

'You know, I was just wondering the same thing. Now and again, it would be possible. Longer term, yes, it could be.'

'You mean she could be hidden within a few feet of us while we're at home, listening when we talk and watching us through a peephole like a mouse behind the plaster. That's weird.'

'Being weird doesn't make something impossible. Have you studied our house?'

'Yes.' Hilda was overtaking a very heavy vehicle and she had to speak up. 'I've swept or scrubbed most of it, but only the inside. If she was squatting in the attic or under the floor, how would she get in and out?'

Michael spoke slowly, racking his memory for details that had faded into the background with time. 'There's no way to get into the underfloor space except by lifting the trap which is in the bottom of the mat well. She could only do that without being heard if we were out of the house. But the attic space is something else again. If you have a good look at the outside of the house you may see that it wasn't all built at the same time. It began as two small cottages. Then somebody incorporated the bit where the kitchen is and the bathroom. It must have been a stable or a cattle-shed originally. The space above there had been used as a hay store. There was a trapdoor over what was the bathroom for shovelling feed through.'

153

'You mean somebody could look through while I'm in the bath?' Hilda asked indignantly.

'If he cared to pull out about forty nails. But the bathroom was moved into the little extension. I nailed the trapdoor up thoroughly and there weren't any chinks. Then when the kitchen was redone I plaster boarded the ceiling. If anybody's using it now, they must get in and out through the wooden door in the gable.'

Hilda was struggling. 'I haven't seen a wooden door.'

'You wouldn't. It's away above your eye level, it's not very big and it's much the same colour as the stonework round about. There's a piece of garden wall left – I think it used to separate the gardens when the place was two cottages. Someone could easily climb up and down by that. I know they could because I've done it. That was easier than fetching out a ladder every time I wanted something that was stored up there. When it was a hayloft the hay would have come in by cart or trailer and that would have brought the load much of the way up. And if that's what she's doing it would explain why everybody's still running around like headless chickens and they all seem sure that we're giving her refuge. It would also explain how your sister came to meet somebody, giving rise to her comment that she didn't think much of the company we keep.'

'She probably came to resume the quarrel. That does seem to add up even if it's what we called it, weird. So what do we do? Phone Honey?'

'Is that what you want to do?'

Hilda thought about it. 'No,' she said. 'Muriel Greening was kind when I hurt myself. I wouldn't want to ... I suppose *betray* is too strong a word but that's the way it feels. At least I'd like to hear her side of the story first. If she's been unlucky, that's one thing; if she's done something awful that's quite different, but I don't believe it. She has a face that's ... not just friendly, not virtuous or angelic, but nice, to use a word I know you despise but which has a real meaning. Do you believe that people who look alike think and behave alike?'

'I'm sure of it. Whole books have been written on the subject. Somatotypes, I think they call it.'

'Well, she looks like people I've known and trusted and who didn't let me down.'

A large car tore past and they rocked in its wake. They let the subject drop for the moment. One or two minor topics came and went but mostly they sat and let the scenery go past. They lunched near the ring road. As they passed Tranent and were nearly home, Michael, who had taken the wheel again, said, 'We'll see if we can arrive home quietly and surprise our uninvited guest – if we have one. Paul Penicuik must have given up keeping observation by now.'

Hilda leaned over and kissed his cheek. 'I knew that there was a soft centre somewhere inside there,' she said.

As they passed the de-restriction sign Michael slipped the car out of gear and coasted. With the last of their momentum he freewheeled into a field gateway. They got out of the car. 'Suppose the farmer comes along,' Hilda said.

'He won't.' Michael nodded toward the field. 'It's already been seeded and rolled.'

They locked the car. Russet, who could not yet be trusted to remain quietly at heel, was left inside and firmly told to wait in silence. They walked along the grass verge, tiptoed across the side road and approached the house. After braving more than a hundred winters and having had many owners it did, as Hilda had said, have a second-hand look, but they loved it.

In a whisper, Michael pointed out that the dividing wall, which had once been the outside gable, held the chimney and so the attic space would never be quite cold. At the gable he pointed to the small door up near the peak. Towards the back corner was a buttress, left when a garden wall was taken down and finishing, to judge by the neatly squared stones, where there had once been a gateway. Michael had never had the heart to take it down because of a handsome Virginia creeper that clad it. That autumn the creeper was a blaze of colour but there were signs of damage to some of the fronds.

Back at the car, Russet was pushing her nose into the narrow window opening that had been left for her comfort. She tried whining but nobody came, so she began levering at the opening with her long nose. There was a hole in the stonework where the latch of the gate had been and another higher up. Traces of mud suggested that these had been used as steps. Doing as little damage to the creeper as possible, Michael repeated a climb that he had often made during his first occupation of the property and was soon standing on top of the wall with the threshold of the wooden door on about the level of his navel. He looked round but this part of the house was not to be seen from Mayview Lodge. He rapped suddenly with his knuckles. 'Come on out,' he said. There was an immediate intensification of the silence as though somebody had stopped breathing but he decided that it was the result of the wildlife taking fright at the sound of his voice. An uncertainty ran up his back at the unknown nature of what was to follow. He knocked again and forced his voice to remain steady. 'Come on out,' he repeated, 'or we'll call the police.'

This time the sounds were more positive and were easily identified. Somebody got to their feet, slipped shoes on and came to the door. There was some fumbling with bolts and a latch. The door swung inward with a Gothic creaking. Mrs Greening, blinking in the daylight, was revealed to Michael as being somewhere in her thirties with an affable face and a good figure that still had some of the bounce of youth. Her skin had seen sunshine in the past without being cared for. It was becoming pale now from a troglodyte existence but it had already become meshed with fine lines. Her dark hair was close cropped. She was wearing jeans and a dark sweater.

'Come on down,' Michael said. 'We have to talk.'

'Talk up here where we can't be seen.' Her voice was high and smooth with a trace of an accent that he thought might be London.

Entering to join her might attract any watching eyes. On the other hand, if she stood arguing for long in the doorway she would certainly be seen. You may feel that you have the countryside to yourself at times, but Sod's Law dictates that if you hope to be private you can be sure that there are eyes hidden somewhere. 'Could you manage?' he asked Hilda.

Hilda glanced down. She was wearing her favourite dress, creamy and delicate and restrictive at the knees. 'I'll go and change,' she said. 'If you're still talking when I come back I'll join you and you can tell me what I've missed.'

'We can wait,' Mrs Greening said. She turned back into the dark attic. Michael had his doubts – Hilda would usually demand at least half an hour for such a change. He was wearing his second-best trousers but if he followed Hilda into the house there was no saying where Mrs Greening would be by the time that he returned. He hoisted himself up.

Mrs Greening, he soon saw, had gone to some trouble to make herself comfortable. A large, worn and grubby carpet, which he had left rolled up in the attic in case he ever wanted to use it for underlay, had been rolled out and nearly covered the worn, oak boards. It would have served to muffle any noises that she made. Even the sound of her kettle boiling would be minimized by being on a rubber mat and in a cardboard box. It and a table lamp were plugged into a socket that Michael had installed when he was moving in and using the attic as a makeshift workshop and store. There was an airbed with a sleeping bag; and a moulded foam armchair had been brought in for daytime use. The roof was of rough boarding with the slater's nails showing through. It was rather like a rough sketch of a comfortable room. It smelled of dust and, despite the warm chimney, it was cold.

As host, Michael felt obliged to gesture her into the chair. Rather than lower himself onto the airbed he remained standing but the limited headroom soon gave him a crick in the neck. He squatted.

'You occupied the house while we were abroad?' he asked.

'Yes.' She seemed to be on the verge of an apology or a request for retrospective permission but decided not to bother.

'Did you meet another woman here?' He could still not bring himself to refer to Estelle as a lady.

It seemed that Mrs Greening had the same reservation. 'There was a woman arrived at the door one day just as I was going out to come back up here. A snooty type. She tried to speak to me but I just nodded and walked on. She looked at me as though I had no business there – which, of course, I hadn't.'

'Nor had she,' Michael said.

Muriel Greening half smiled. 'Didn't she? I wish I'd known that at the time. I could have given her back look for look.'

Hilda, determined not to miss a syllable, could be heard outside. Michael, equally determined that his Virginia creeper be spared avoidable damage, reached down from the doorway, gripped her wrist and helped her inside. Hilda appeared to have changed into jeans and a jumper to match Mrs Greening's and then to have combed her hair with her fingers while making a hurried return. By tacit consent Hilda took the armchair, Michael sank uncomfortably onto the airbed and Mrs Greening, being the shortest, remained standing.

'Now,' Michael said, 'you'd better tell us what this is about.'

Mrs Greening looked at him blankly. 'If you don't know, you can't expect me to tell you,' she said.

'Then I'll start you off.' Michael was realizing that he already had some of the strands at the forefront of his mind. 'You're a gambler,' he said. Mrs Greening flushed and bit her lip. 'In a small way, probably,' he resumed. 'But that kind of betting can get out of hand. I've seen it before among friends of mine. Losses accumulate. Credit gets extended. Somebody whispers that the luck will surely turn and if you increase the stakes you'll clear the debt.' Mrs Greening was looking out of the doorway towards the twisted limbs of an ancient pine tree but Michael was in no doubt that he was hitting the mark. 'Please remember that we're on your side. You were kind to Hilda when she hurt her ankle so we've been protecting you. If you're frank with us, we may be able to go on doing so.

'A gambling debt isn't recoverable at law so you would be made to sign IOUs and when the crunch came it would be pointed out that the IOUs didn't say anything about gambling. You would also be threatened with violence.

'And now I'm guessing, but I suspect that pressure was put on your husband to pay up. And until he did or could, you went into hiding. Yes?' Mrs Greening lowered her eyes and remained dumb. 'But Mr Greening has a senior job, he makes good money. He could manage a small to medium sum without difficulty. Was he being pushed for more than he could manage?'

'Not money,' she said. 'It wasn't that. I think they doctored my IOUs before they showed them to him. I know I hadn't lost that much. But they threatened to beat me up if the debt wasn't settled. Gordon wouldn't stand by for that – he's very protective. And they wouldn't take money, even when he offered it although it would have hurt. He's only just been promoted into his present job but he says we'll soon be in the black. He pretended he could raise enough but they knew about his interest.'

Michael was prepared to go on guessing although he was passing from fact to wild speculation. 'Which of his various interests was that?'

Mrs Greening had had enough. Standing, she had what amounted to a flying start. Getting up from the very low airbed was difficult and, by the time that Michael had managed to rise, Mrs Greening had darted to the doorway, found her first foothold and made a leap to the ground. With an unexpected athleticism, she rolled and came back to her feet.

Russet chose that moment to arrive at the lollop, the car's window having yielded. She swerved towards Mrs Greening, gave a short bark of welcome and made to jump up. The lady leaped back, gave the dog a push with her foot that was almost a kick and took to her heels. They heard her splash through the boggy ground beyond their back fence but by the time they were both down she was gone and not even a sound was left behind to be followed. Russet stood looking at where the fleeing figure had vanished, her whole posture expressive of wounded feelings. There would, it seemed, be no more tasty bribes from that quarter.

THIRTEEN

The house seemed cold and empty when they let themselves in after their weekend's absence. That reminded Michael of the occasions when they had been surprised to find a piece of equipment mildly warm and they had suspected that current had been arriving via a short circuit or a freak of induction. He followed Hilda into the kitchen. It had never before occurred to them that somebody else might be using their facilities in their absence but now they were noticing small signs where some implement was not quite where it had been left.

'Do we know any financial whizz-kids?' Michael asked. 'It would have been useful if once upon a time I'd produced a family tree for Bill Gates or Richard Branson, to serve as an introduction. I can only make sense of what's been going on if I assume that there's bigger money at stake than a housewife's losses on the horses. But it can all make sense if her husband's either rolling in it or in a position to pull off a really major fraud. Any criminal might then want to hold your friend to ransom.'

'I see what you mean, but I can't think of anybody who'd know that sort of thing,' Hilda said. 'Except my dad. He always seems to know what's going on in the world of moolah.'

'Great! Ring him up and ask if he knows or can find out what jiggery-pokery might be going on at Quimbles. Emphasize that extreme discretion is called for.'

While Hilda phoned her father, Michael made the attic, the former hayloft, secure against uninvited guests. Mrs Greening would have to come to the front door if she wished to recover any of her property. There was some of her clothing that had been left behind when she fled, and some cosmetics including a small bottle of the perfume that Hilda had so much disliked. When he returned to the sitting room, Hilda had finished her call and seemed pleased. 'He knows just the person – a man who he says is a much bigger fish in the financial puddle and always seems to know everything before anyone else. I made him promise to be as discreet as he possibly could.'

'That's all right, then.'

But it was not all right. Next morning, breakfast was hardly over when DCI Honey Laird arrived on the doorstep, accompanied by an Inspector Dodson. Both officers looked stern. Rather than be invited to come for interview to the nearest police station, which seemed to be high on the possible agenda, Michael took them into the sitting room and invited them to sit. Hilda hurried to join the party.

Honey refused the offer of refreshments and did not waste words on preliminaries. Greetings did not seem to be called for and she was less than interested in anyone's health. 'Why do you want to know about finances at Quimbles?'

Trading a question for a question with the police is not usually a satisfactory procedure but Michael decided to try it anyway. 'How do you know...?'

He was not even allowed to finish his enquiry. 'I'll ask the questions,' Honey snapped.

Michael was about to say that he had as much right to ask questions as she had when it occurred to him that this was probably not so. On the other hand, he had just as much right to be infuriating and Honey was beginning to put his back up. He looked at Hilda. 'While I deal with the officers,' he said, 'please phone your father and ask him who he consulted.'

Hilda pretended to be on the point of rising. Honey snorted. If a beautiful woman could be said to glare, she glared. 'Don't bother,' she ground out. 'Mr Gilmour phoned Mr Potterton-Phipps.'

Michael remembered that Honeypot had been born Honoria Potterton-Phipps, hence the sobriquet. 'Your father,' he said.

'My father,' she confirmed. 'And probably just as well for you, because you were getting into deep and muddy waters. Now tell me what you know and how you came to know it.'

It was obvious that Honey was ready to bite, and her position in the police gave her the teeth to bite with. Michael decided once again that the time had come for frankness. 'I don't know anything for sure. But I figured that with so much going on there had to be more to it than the gambling debts of a housewife.' There was a pause while Michael applied a little censorship to the next part of the tale. 'There seemed to be a general assumption that she was drawn to this house and spending at least some time here. Hilda's sister said that she tried to visit us while we were still away and there she bumped into another caller, a woman. Then I remembered that there was a small, disused hayloft over what had once been a stable or a byre but became the kitchen and bathroom area and the walk-in airing cupboard. It's all kitchen now. The external doorway is high up in the gable and very inconspicuous and tends to be forgotten about. The internal opening down which they used to drop hay for the beasts was nailed up long before I came here, but I thought I should take a look at the attic.'

Honey's air of disapproval doubled. 'It did not occur to you that looking at it might be my job?'

Michael adopted the tone that Hilda used when she had decided that he was being particularly obtuse. 'Chief Inspector,' he said gently, 'I seem to recall that you asked us, once upon a time, to keep an eye open for places where Mrs Greening might be hiding out. We were hoping to do as you asked and to give you a helping hand. You wouldn't have thanked us if we had sent you on one fool's errand after another. The public are always being asked to help the police but when we do it we get our bottoms smacked.'

If the soft answer turned away any of Honey's wrath there was little or no sign of it. 'Which never seems to teach you or them anything. Let me tell you what happened next. You found Mrs Greening in possession. If you had held onto her, I like to think that you'd have called me or my colleagues, but I can't be sure. You didn't, so I can only conclude that she gave you the slip. Correct?'

Hilda and Michael exchanged a rueful glance. 'Very close,' Hilda said.

'But not before you got something out of her? Something that induced you to start making your own, unofficial enquiries?'

Michael had no reason to be friendly towards Estelle, the woman who had knocked him cold and then accused him without any reason whatever of collecting child pornography. But she was Hilda's sister. That might normally have entitled her to a little consideration but she had a history of being unkind to Hilda. Also she was to be the subject of a far more artistic revenge. If the faked family tree failed to put Estelle to shame, that would be time enough to unmask her as the culprit who had wasted police time with false accusations. 'Not a word,' he said. 'To be honest, I did the talking, but my guess still is that her husband had been under pressure to make good her gambling debts. Presumably the threats were of violence to her and she had faded out of sight while he gathered up the money. I wondered how he was raising a substantial sum and whether it was the method of raising it that was the real objective. When I began to suggest as much, she bolted, which suggested that I was coming close to the truth.'

'And now,' Honey said grimly, 'you are patting yourself on the back for gathering up on my behalf a little fact and a lot of speculation that we already had. And in

172

doing so you've chased her out of a place where she may have been relatively safe and into deadly danger.'

'You've no reason to suppose such a thing,' Michael said hotly.

'Have I not? Think about this. There are some very ruthless citizens mixed up in this. Not Penicuik, your local bookie. You remember Alec Jenkinson?'

'I heard him mentioned, once or twice.'

'A nice, innocent-sounding name, isn't it? Don't let that fool you into thinking of him as in any way nice or innocent. His main business, in Glasgow, the one that he started off with, is gambling of all sorts. But everything is a gamble, at least everything to do with money, and a successful bookie has the money to bankroll – as my American colleagues put it – all sorts of crime. It follows inevitably that he can then gather around him some very tough hangers-on who have every incentive to ensure that anything that the boss is financing comes out in profit. Thanks to you, Mrs Greening has nowhere to go now.

'I'll tell you a little more, because you could probably piece it together if you went on consulting Mr Gilmour as your oracle and asking questions; and also because I want you to realize that this is serious. I simply cannot run any risk of you saying the wrong thing to the wrong person. I'm working with the Scottish Crime and Drugs Enforcement Agency on this and if you breathe a word outside present company they'll have you for breakfast.

'About seven weeks ago an officer about to go on duty was walking his dog along the banks of the Thames and he made a shocking discovery. He thought at first that he had found a body, obviously murdered. He called for help immediately. Luckily the police surgeon was nearby and he got to the scene quickly. He was on the ball and detected faint signs of life. The man was given every possible care. Every effort was made to resuscitate him, but he soon died. Not, however, before he had made a deathbed statement. He had a dozen broken bones, mostly by crushing, and he had been stabbed several times and worked over with a blowlamp.'

The horror of such a death struck home to both her listeners. Honey continued into a silence that was absolute.

'It's a sad story. We've managed to keep it quiet so far and it must stay like that, so I won't say the man's name aloud. He was no saint but he didn't deserve what happened. His wife disappeared. He traced her, eventually, but too late. She'd been drawn into a particular web of vice at the centre of which is a man known as Mr Sweet, solely because that bears some resemblance to his Latvian name. There is nothing else sweet about him. He was the death of her. There's no point going into details; just take my word for it.

'There was nothing left for him to wish for except revenge. He approached a police officer and was passed on up the chain. The upshot was that a regular informant was paid to introduce him to Mr Sweet. He was a skilled forger so his services on such things as stolen passports were welcomed. He soon heard that something big was brewing. It had been brought to Alec Jenkinson by Paul Penicuik and Jenkinson had decided that it was too big to be handled from Glasgow and so he took it to Mr Sweet. He gathered that it was a potentially huge fraud which would be perpetrated over the Internet and would be quite untraceable, but that it wasn't quite within their grasp yet. Even within Sweet's organization it was only mentioned in whispers, but the two names that he caught were Haddington and Greening.

'Naturally a watch was established but there's been no sign of a new Internet fiddle. For years it has been possible to hack into the computer of a bank, a billionaire or a wealthy company. It happened often, but electronic transactions leave traces. It was possible to route the messages over a mobile phone and through somebody else's computer, but that usually only makes it more difficult, not impossible, to trace. It may be that they have already pulled it off but that the fraud has not yet been discovered; but if that's so, why are they still running around trying to put pressure on Frank Greening?'

'But what's so special about Mr Greening?' Hilda asked, struggling to hide her shock.

'Mr Greening is one of those men who think in binary arithmetic and computer language. It's what he does. And his hobby is hacking. Not for profit and he has no truck with viruses, but because to him hacking is fun. He enjoys breaking into other people's Internet traffic and seeing what's going on, and if he picks up a little valuable commercial information along the way, so much the better. Sometimes he leaves behind an insulting message just to let them know that they've been penetrated. Any comment so far? You used to be an IT consultant so you should know what I'm talking about.'

Michael came out of a momentary trance. 'I would have said that it was impossible to do something so big and to leave no recoverable traces. It might be done through some devious route that left the traces where they would never be found, but they would still exist. Most commonly, things that people believe have been eradicated from a computer are merely unavailable because normal means of accessing them have gone. If you're telling me that such traces simply no longer exist, have been totally eliminated and all traces of that elimination have similarly vanished totally, then, if I believe you, somebody with inside knowledge and more expertise than I ever had has discovered the key to El Dorado. And, yes, I can see that to a ruthless gang it would look like the end of the rainbow.'

Honey nodded. 'Now perhaps you'll see the reasons why you must remain silent on the subject and take no actions that might rock the official boat. You'll notice that neither Inspector Dodson nor I have been taking notes and we have no recording devices with us. The matter is too confidential for any record to be made. There is now no sign of Mrs Greening and we suspect that she may have been kidnapped. If not, she soon may be. And then her life may hang by a thread. She must know who is threatening her; and these people are not known for leaving witnesses alive. In fact, I can put it more strongly. The reason that we have never got close to them is that witnesses who might have sunk them have a habit of disappearing as completely and mysteriously as the traces that we've been discussing. If Mrs Greening is still alive it is because Jenkinson and his hangers-on still hope to squeeze the secret program out of her husband – who, I may say, has a sideline in writing uncopiable computer programs for games manufacturers and others.'

Hilda had been listening to this exchange, her eyes flicking from one speaker to the other like a spectator at a tennis match; but anyone familiar enough with her expressions might have realized that she was coming to the boil. 'I think you've got a bloody nerve,' she said suddenly. 'Ticking Mike off for trying to help you when you'd asked for his help and if you'd been a bit more forthcoming in the first place we'd have known that she was in danger and how far we could go trying to help you and what we shouldn't do if we happened to come across where Mrs Greening was hiding out.' She paused for breath. 'You asked us to watch out for her. You want to save her because you're an officer of the law and it's your duty; but I like her, I think of her as a friend and it was on that basis that I wanted to help. Why didn't you take her into – what d'you call it? Protective custody.'

Honey's nostrils flared. 'That is exactly what I have been trying to do –' (Michael half-expected to have to referee a hair-pulling bout at any moment) '– and if you had told me about your attic when I first came enquiring, protective custody is exactly where she would be.'

Michael decided that it was high time to step between them even if it meant attracting some of the animosity. 'I had quite forgotten about the old hayloft,' he said, 'and Hilda never knew about it. But there's no point exchanging recriminations.'

'Faults on both sides,' said Inspector Dodson. He gave the impression of having his tongue firmly in his cheek and rather enjoying himself.

Michael expected Honey to turn and rend her companion but apparently he had some licence. She swallowed and took a few seconds to cool down. 'That's as may be,' she said at last. 'The damage is done. The question is how to limit the risk.'

'If there's any way that we can help to bring Mrs Greening out of danger,' Michael said, 'just tell us.'

It was Honeypot's turn to adopt the tone and cadence usually reserved for communication with children or the mentally retarded. 'I still don't seem to have got through to you. I can't force you to walk around with your eyes tight shut. If I could, I would. If

180

you happen to learn anything of possible significance, phone me or get a message to me through any police office. Do nothing whatever else, you understand?'

'I think we can puzzle out your meaning,' Michael said, tight-lipped. 'But there's just one other thing. When I had my confrontation with Brian Foley, Mr Penicuik's gofer, I told him that he was making a mistake with his gardening. He started consulting me. Shall I follow up the connection?'

'On no account. And if he should approach you for more advice, give it, but that's absolutely all. Got it? Good. Then if you'll let us into your loft we'll see what goodies Mrs Greening may have left behind.'

Michael handed over the key to his padlock. 'There's a light switch just inside the door on your right. Return the key to me when you leave.'

'Quite possibly,' Honey said, 'Mrs Greening may return in the hope of collecting some of her things.' Her eyes glinted as she saw her chance to teach Inspector Dodson a lesson about pulling the legs of his superiors. 'Inspector Dodson will remain on watch in the attic until further notice. No doubt you will allow him the use of your facilities.'

Hilda said, 'If he pays us a call before he settles down, we'll acquaint him with the house rules.'

Inspector Dodson only grinned.

FOURTEEN

At breakfast, Hilda looked as though her sleep had been restless. There were dark thumbprints under her eyes and her eyelids drooped. Michael decided to drag the subject into the open by asking what was disturbing her. She choked off a yawn and said that she couldn't put Muriel Greening out of her mind.

'To that Honeypot woman she's just a piece in a big board game. It's all very well telling us to go away and play. But Muriel's too nice and friendly a person to turn our backs on. I think she would only have started betting on the horses because she was bored and short of company during the day. Perhaps I should have looked in on her now and again. Most of the women in that part of the village go out to work in Quimbles. If we really have put her in danger...' She was forced to break off, having filled her mouth with toast. Anxiety had not affected her appetite.

'She was already in danger,' Michael pointed out. 'If Detective Chief Inspector Laird is to be believed, which is far from certain. I wouldn't put it past that dragon to exaggerate the danger for her own ends.'

Hilda chewed hastily and swallowed. 'That doesn't help much. It's still true that she was hiding out in our attic for fear of something and we more or less chased her out to take her chances in a hostile world. Would the police still be watching her house?'

'Yesterday I'd have thought not, because continuous surveillance is so expensive both in time and money that they have to fill out great long forms and get special permission even to think about it. But we didn't realize then how seriously they were taking it. There could be a lot more money involved than the cost of one surveillance team. So yes, I'm sure her house is being watched.'

'That leaves her with nowhere to go,' Hilda said. She sounded tearful. 'I can imagine her sleeping rough last night but by

184

now she'll be cold and hungry. She probably won't have the skills to look after herself and stay out of trouble.'

Michael could see the direction that her thoughts were taking and he did not like it. 'The more police are watching the less likely it is that anyone can get at her. We can't do anything,' he said. 'Honeypot made it clear that she would be very annoyed if we interfered again and I can lead a happier life if I avoid annoying senior police officers.'

Hilda lifted her chin. 'She knows that we have a dog to walk and she said that if we came across anything relevant we were to let her know. Also she knows that Mr Penicuik's gardener is consulting you. So she could hardly be surprised if we happened to see whatever was happening at Mayview Lodge from a distance while we're walking Russet.' Recognizing her name, Russet thumped the carpet twice with her tail. 'I can't think of any other steps we could usefully take, can you?'

Feeling his argument slipping away from him, Michael weakened. He loved Hilda dearly and hated to refuse her anything. 'I suppose we could watch from the hill,' he

185

said, 'in case she turns up there, though I can't imagine why she should or what we'd do if she did. But that would be on the clear understanding that if we see anything we call Honeypot.'

Hilda jumped to her feet, kissed him on the ear and then hurried to the kitchen worktop. 'Now what are you up to?' he asked patiently.

'We can't just walk past, give a quick glance and go home,' she pointed out. 'If anything significant is going to happen there, we'll need to be there to see it. I'm making sandwiches. If you want to help, you could do the dishes. Pâté or egg and cress?'

Accepting Hilda's argument, it followed that an early move was to be desired. After an interval spent scurrying around and falling over each other they amazed themselves by being established, well before mid-morning, in a sheltered and hidden nook between two broom bushes. They were equipped with sandwiches, vacuum flasks, Russet's dinner, binoculars and the camera. In addition to Michael's mobile phone Hilda had brought out and put on charge, for the duration of their preparations, an older mobile, rarely used because of its weight and bulk. While Hilda finished the sandwiches, Michael had taken a walk past Cairncross Cottage. Different car, different man, but the same meticulous observation.

They had soon settled into a routine of taking turnabout for half an hour at a time, one of them watching Mayview Lodge while the other gave Russet a short walk and then relaxed.

Watching nothing can be very hard work. Even the sight of Brian Foley, dead-heading rhododendrons until a short shower drove him indoors, added little interest. The traffic of pigeons and crows soon petered out. Several rabbits came out to feed or to play. Two of them mated, but that spectacle was short-lived. Hilda, though still sleepy, had brightened up now that they were taking action. 'You needn't think that *you* could get away with such a short performance,' Hilda said. 'Not that I'm complaining. You never do rush it.'

'Some things are too good to hurry.'

'I'm really glad that you said that. Are the police watching here – and if not, why not?'

'They can't watch everywhere at the same time and the only place with a proven link to the Greenings is their house.'

At half past noon they began on their sandwiches and by twelve-forty they had finished them. The day crawled onward. Michael was on the point of calling it a day and going home to change his slightly damp clothing when Hilda, whose turn it was to watch, said, 'Something's happening.'

Michael put aside his mug of coffee, crawled up beside her and looked. Even a pair of mating frogs would have been preferable to the monumental boredom of watching eternally for something unspecified that never happened. This was not a great deal better. Against the nearer wall of the house was planted a lean-to double garage, an afterthought in concrete slab construction. The double door was rising, apparently by magic and of its own accord, revealing the backs of two cars. Beyond, a pair of gates was similarly swinging open on a driveway that led to the end of the village street. The scene dozed again but the black void of the garage doorway was drawing the eye.

Fifteen tedious minutes ground by. Michael was observing while Hilda gave Russet a comfort break among the bushes. A pale van turned off the village street and entered the drive. It came to a halt on the gravel outside the garage. Brian Foley came out of the house to confer with another figure from the van. Some gestures were visible and once Brian nodded in the direction of the hill. Michael had been giving some thought to possible scenarios and these visible signs fitted neatly into one of them. On a sudden hunch he backed away from the brink of the hill and hurried for fifty paces before lowering himself and crawling to where he could rise and peer out through the branches of a thick holly tree.

His hunch had been sound. The van, with its rear doors open, had been reversed in a quarter-circle and was coming to rest in the garage doorway. From their earlier observation post the van would have cut off his view but from this angle he could see into a segment of the garage. It was a limited view and not well lit, but what he saw set him groping for his mobile phone. Honeypot had given him her mobile number and that of Inspector Dodson and each was listed in the memory of each of their mobile phones. He keyed her number.

It was engaged. He looked up to the heavens and tried Dodson's number. This time he got an answer. He identified himself and began his report.

'Hold your horses,' said the inspector's voice. 'This is the chief inspector's own case and she won't be pleased if I interfere unnecessarily.'

'But she isn't answering her mobile. She's talking on it. Can't you relay a message? She couldn't call that interference, or unnecessary.'

'I'm not going to be a post office. Hold the line for a moment.' The moment stretched out into many moments and Michael was ready to gibber with impatience before the inspector's Highland lilt came back on the line. 'I called her on the radio. She'll call you back as soon as she's free.'

Michael waited. He realized suddenly that Hilda was standing silent beside him. Her eyebrows had almost disappeared under her hairline. 'What gives?' she asked. 'I had a hell of a job finding you.'

'That's reassuring. I couldn't have seen

from where we were.' His mobile played a short little melody from the score of some ballet. 'Just listen and you'll know as much as I do.' Honey's voice came on the phone, sounding querulous. 'I'm on the hill behind Mayview Lodge,' Michael said into the phone.

'I thought I told you—'

'You never said that we mustn't walk the dog. Do you want my report or don't you?'

'Go ahead.' Her tone said *this had better be good.*

'About ten minutes ago a van, pale grey I think, came to the house. The garage double door had been opened. The van with its rear doors ajar was backed up to the opening of the garage door. Three people got out of the back of the van and went into the garage. My view was largely cut off by the van's doors but I could see their legs from the calf down. I gained the impression of two men with a woman between them.'

'What gave you that impression?'

'I had already seen two men. The outer two figures walked like men, firmly and with longer strides. The middle legs were more slender and the feet walked more lightly. I think the shoe heels were higher. The walk was irregular, as if she was being pulled along, stumbling. The van has now driven off.' He quoted the registration number.

'And you're sure you're not letting your imagination run away with you?'

'Quite sure.'

'You say that you'd already seen two men?'

'One of them was Brian Foley. The other was very tall and thin and bald.'

'Now you begin to carry conviction.' There was a silence on the line. When she spoke again she had had time for thought. Her voice was firmer. 'It's very tenuous. On what we've got, which is little more than your impression of a distant view, I don't think that I could get authority to search against the owner's will, but I'll try. Any wrong move could put her life in real danger – if it isn't already. I'll also put together a cordon in case it's called for. What you do is nothing. Nothing whatever. Except...'

'Yes?'

'If a vehicle leaves and you believe that she has been put into it, see which way it goes. Follow if you can. Keep in touch with me. Do your best but take no other action.'

Michael was tempted to reply 'dob, dob, dob, dob,' but refrained. They disconnected.

'You heard all that?' Michael asked Hilda, who nodded.

'If we're going to be useful – we do want to be useful?'

'Yes, of course.'

'Then we'll have to get ready. We'll take one mobile each. I'll leave you here with Russet and one of the mobiles – the old one; it won't be fully charged but it can plug into the socket in the car – and go for my bike. You'd better keep the binoculars. I'll try for somewhere inconspicuous just off the road, where I can pull out and follow up whenever you can describe a vehicle that you think may have Mrs Greening as a passenger, willing or unwilling. If we get that far, you and Russet dash home and get your car out. I'll leave the Sat Nav in your car – I can't read it while riding on the motorbike anyway. I'll try to keep you posted and you can follow me up.'

'I think I've got all that,' said Hilda. 'Now you'd better hurry. They could leave at any time.'

'I doubt it. They'll be asking her questions or phoning the big boss for instructions.'

'And suppose the big boss says, "Bring her to me"?'

'You have a point,' Michael said. 'But they're more likely to wait for darkness.' All the same, he hurried away in the direction of home. Suddenly time, which had been dragging, was beginning to fly.

Ten minutes later Hilda received a call. 'Where are my leathers?'

'On a hanger in the hall cupboard. There wasn't room in your wardrobe.'

'Thanks.'

After a further fifteen minutes, the older mobile played its little tune again. 'I'm in place,' Michael said. 'I've got a good view of the front of the house but I don't think I can be seen. There's a track that turns into the small wood on the right just beyond Quimbles. Bring your car there. Unless I phone to warn you, you've time to prepare some more sandwiches. We don't have control of the timetable.'

'The van drove off again. I'm sure it was

the baldy man driving. There was no sign of the woman so she must still be there.'

This time, nearly an hour passed. Infant spiders were spinning webs in the bushes while they waited for a breeze to give them a lift. Michael wondered about the instincts entailed. Then Hilda's car turned into the track, bumped over ruts that had remained untouched since the previous winter and came to rest beside the Suzuki. Michael was relieved that the charge in the mobile's battery had lasted – that had been a weak point in his plan but the mobile was now plugged into the dashboard socket. He settled into the passenger seat and borrowed back his binoculars. Nobody seemed to be taking any interest in them. If they had been observed at all they must have been taken for a courting couple, which in a sense they were. A bank topped with gorse hid them from the road and from Mayview Lodge but they had a passable view between the stems.

'I had a call from that Honeypot person,' Hilda said. 'She's on the way here. She thinks she'll be here in about another ten minutes.'

Michael was suddenly alert. 'That may be too late. There's a big Volvo just arrived at the front of the house.'

'Let me see.' Hilda grabbed the binoculars. Michael, luckily, managed to remove the strap from around his neck in time. He keyed Honeypot's number on his own mobile and fidgeted until she answered.

The DCI's voice came on the line. 'A large estate car has just arrived at Mayview Lodge,' Michael reported, 'and a bundle was put into the back. It may have been old laundry but it could just as easily have been a body or a person bound.'

'Registration and make?'

'Volvo.' He snatched back the binoculars and quoted the registration number.

'Hold the line.' There was a long pause while Honeypot referred to Swansea for the owner's identity. 'Well done!' The praise sounded ungrudging. 'This is what we want.'

'If you're nearly here...' Michael said. 'Hang on ... yes, they're leaving and they've turned towards Edinburgh. If you're nearing here, you may meet them.'

'Except that I'm coming from the other

side, from Duns. You'll have to follow, but for God's sake don't be seen.'

Michael disconnected and opened his door. 'Somebody seems to have suffered a sea change. Whatever happened to "Watch and do nothing whatever else"? You follow them. Stay far enough back not to worry them. I'll be behind you on the Suzuki. If either of us thinks there's any danger of you being spotted I'll overtake you. If we change places now and again it may disarm his suspicions.'

'Well, you be careful,' Hilda said. 'If he does spot us he may not be pleased, and I wouldn't fancy your chances on the motorbike in a shunt with the Volvo.'

'No more would I. But the motorbike's more manoeuvrable. I can keep out of his way. You're probably more vulnerable than I am.'

'Believe me,' Hilda said, 'I'll be careful enough for two.'

FIFTEEN

Hilda bumped her car over the ruts and reached the mouth of the track just as a large van emblazoned with the name of the local removals firm passed by. She swore aloud but soon realized that the van, rather than being an obstruction, was a useful concealment. She lurched out and followed it patiently, judging the gap by the shadow of the Volvo. Occasional glimpses of her target assured her that she was, quite literally, shadowing the right vehicle. The spaceman figure of Michael on his Suzuki in leathers, helmet and visor remained small in her mirror.

The van was bombing along, but a high-mileage LDV van was no match for a nearly new Volvo. Hilda had the advantage of knowing most of the roads thereabouts, but when the gap between the van and the Volvo stretched to the point where she was in danger of being caught out by sudden junctions, she was forced to overtake the van and match her pace to that of the Volvo, although remaining a long way behind. Michael followed suit. Would somebody in the car spot that they were being followed? Hilda wished she knew whether the bald man was alone. The sun was reflecting from the Volvo's rear window so that there could have been a gorilla in the passenger seat and she would not have known. Driving on these roads he would not dare to take his eyes off the road for long enough to study the traffic in his mirror. Minutes later, it seemed that Michael felt the same unease. He drew closer and when conditions of road and traffic permitted he pulled out and thrust past. Hilda could drop back and keep Michael in sight but be invisible from the Volvo.

They were into the network of minor roads lying between Dalkeith and the Moorfoot Hills. The roads were narrow. They twisted, forked and joined again. She was soon sure that the other driver was choosing his route not because it was the nearest to his destination but because a follower would be easier to detect or to evade. Entering a road that memory insisted ran straighter than most, she pulled over, keyed the digits for DCI Laird's mobile and passed on their present coordinates.

Michael had taken over following the Volvo but when he was screened by a leafy bend a Range Rover overtook him with a crisp exhaust note that sounded very different from a standard Range Rover. He recognized Honeypot, alone in the vehicle, making signals at him. Hoping that he was interpreting them correctly he dropped back to let her go by and take up the pursuit.

They happened to be in an area that he knew comparatively well because he had often entered clay-pigeon shooting competitions in an abandoned quarry there during his bachelor days. He was beginning to retreat into a daydream about the last such occasion, when he had found form and shot to Olympic standard for a glorious afternoon. He would definitely have triumphed but for a sudden gust of wind that had tweaked his penultimate clay out from the sweep of his shot pattern. After that, he had missed his last target by a wide margin.

He was wrenched back to the present when the Range Rover pulled onto a grassy area beside a minor crossroads. Honeypot got out, still talking into a hand-held radio, and waved him down. 'Lost him,' she said in exasperation. 'Think he knew he was being followed. You've got a mobile. Race ahead and see if you overtake him. I'll send your lady love left and I'll try to the right myself when I've called for support. Go!' She was speaking again into her personal radio before he could even get into gear.

Michael blasted ahead, but he was not hopeful. He remembered the road ahead as leading into a tangle of minor roads and farm tracks. At the same time he was rejoicing in the excuse to race along the twisting roads, secure in the knowledge that he was acting on the orders of a senior police officer. He reached a crest from which he could see at least a mile ahead. The road was blocked by a tractor that was trying to manoeuvre a trailer-load of overhanging straw bales through a narrow gate. The process seemed to have been in train for some time and looked likely to continue indefinitely. The Volvo could certainly not have passed that place in the time. To the right he could see the edge of the sprawl of Edinburgh and the bright water of the River Forth beyond.

He leaned, turned and hastened back to the crossroads. Honeypot's Range Rover was where he had last seen it but with two maps on the bonnet, weighted down with stones, and her Sat Nav between. It had been joined by Hilda's small saloon and the two women were standing together.

'Tall, thin and bald,' the DCI was saying into her radio. 'He's believed to be alone. He is Clive Spicer and he works for Alec Jenkinson. He looks innocent enough but he's a bad, rough, cruel beggar, so don't take any chances and don't tackle him without back-up. One thing, he probably is not heeled, guns aren't his thing, but watch out for a knife. And one other thing – I'm told that he's a coward.'

Hilda had brought sandwiches, hastily but generously prepared by scooping chopped tomatoes and the last of the pâté into split and buttered rolls. There were two large flasks of coffee. It seemed a good moment to open the package and begin to eat. Michael put the bike on its stand, removed his helmet and sat back on the saddle beside the open door of Hilda's car. Honeypot finished giving the coordinates of a roundabout to be watched. She fetched her shooting stick out of the Range Rover, snapped it open with an angry gesture and joined them, accepting a sandwich and a paper napkin. There were only two mugs but Michael made do with the cap of one of the two flasks. Their picnic place was sheltered by a row of mature beeches and warm in the autumn sun although the treetops were stirred by a breeze.

'Don't blame yourselves,' the DCI said. There was more sympathy in her voice than Michael had previously heard. 'It takes several cars and a lot of special training plus a thorough briefing before a suspicious target can be followed without knowing it. Even so, it's tricky unless you can plant a homing bug in his vehicle.'

'Which is all very well,' Hilda said, 'but what have we done to Muriel Greening's chances?'

They were interrupted, apparently to

Honeypot's relief, by the arrival of Sergeant Grant in a small police Ford. The grassy triangle was becoming crowded. The sergeant was given a protracted briefing and sent to sit in the Range Rover to monitor the radio traffic. He seemed disappointed not to have been offered a sandwich.

'I could only make a wild guess about Mrs Greening's chances,' Honey finally replied. 'This is not the kind of thing that one would usually discuss with a member of the public, but you're a friend of hers and you've made an effort to help us to help her. I'll just say this. Now that we've let them know that we're after them, her chances are a lot worse than they were. But removing her from Mayview Lodge in daylight suggests that she was still alive and that the top dog wants to question her. That looks hopeful.'

They took what comfort they could from that. There was nothing to say, not much to think about. Michael tried to count the starlings gathering on telegraph wires at the roadside, preparing for their migration. Honeypot's radio quacked occasionally with a report of nothing much. Crows, heading for their roosts, plodded by high overhead.

The radio came alive. The Volvo had been seen but it had turned back. Presumably the driver's suspicions had been aroused. Then it was seen again, approaching a different roadblock, but that turned out to be the wrong car. A man in a big Vauxhall was seen driving erratically, possibly drunk, but the order was given to make a report but otherwise to ignore him. Honeypot bent over her maps and issued some crisp orders. All went quiet again.

With a suddenness that made Hilda's heart jump, a voice broke through. 'Here he comes,' and then, 'Got him! He ran over a stinger and tried to keep going with two flats, lost control and went over an embankment. Car's a write-off and he's bust a leg and an arm.'

'Then you'd better hope and pray that it was the right Volvo,' Honeypot said.

'My God, Guv! Don't even think such a thing.' The voice sounded less exultant. There was silence for a few seconds. 'It's OK; I just checked the number plate again.'

'Was there a woman in the car?'

'He was alone.'

'Ask him where she is.'

There was another delay. 'He isn't saying a word, Guv. Just presses his lips tight together and pretends to be unconscious. There's an ambulance on the way.'

Michael was shaking Honeypot's arm. 'Tell him to stick his head in the back of the car and sniff. Quickly before it disperses in the breeze.'

'I heard that,' said the disembodied voice. 'Hang on a jiff.'

Honeypot sighed. 'It's time that Sergeant Rose was sent on a refresher course in radio procedures. Would Mrs Greening still be using perfume, and the same perfume, while living rough?'

'She was using it when we found her in our attic,' Hilda said. 'She'd need it all the more, living rough.'

Honeypot nodded uncertainly. They gathered that she had never been without bathing facilities.

The voice returned. 'Don't know who you've got with you, Guv, but he's right. Pongs of lilac, I think, with lemons.'

'That's it,' Hilda said.

'Well done, Sergeant,' Honeypot said. She closed the radio and called to Sergeant

206

Grant. 'That's it, Gordon. Tell everybody to stand down but they can't go home yet. We may need a search.'

Honeypot suddenly looked older. Michael decided that her responsibilities were weighing heavily upon her. He said, 'Before you start scouring the countryside – which may be wasting time while her life's in danger – let's just think for a minute. We were never far behind the Volvo until we lost him. But how did we come to lose him?'

'That I can't tell you,' said Honeypot. 'I wasn't far behind him, but it was one of those places where bend follows bend. Suddenly he just wasn't there.'

'I think I can tell you why. Let's have one quick look. I have a hunch. I know just the place.'

Honeypot held his eye for several seconds and then nodded. 'Your hunches have been good so far.'

'Follow me, then.'

Michael, on the Suzuki, led the procession of three cars back to the area from which the Volvo had vanished. He was surprised to find how much his memory for the countryside had faded since, with the arrival of

Hilda, his visits to the clay-pigeon shooting club had ceased. Hilda did not approve of shotguns even when used on inanimate targets, and anyway her arrival on the scene had introduced more enticing challenges than the prospect of an occasional medal. But he recognized an oak tree that was just shedding its leaves and a stone's throw back towards Haddington he found the gap where a tall hedge almost closed overhead. He made a sharp turn round a copse of what he thought were alders. A minute's ride between young silver birches and a well-remembered scene opened up. He was on a vacant area of roughly flattened ground that he remembered seeing cluttered with vehicles and men.

During the process of running out of usable stone, the quarry, which occupied no more than three or four hectares, had been worked at different levels with ramps between. This had become convenient later to the clay-pigeon club when a variety of 'birds' was required for competitions, but it made it more difficult for the would-be rescuers to be sure that the unfortunate lady had not been rolled out of the Volvo and over one of the drops. Michael however called on what remained of his memory. A vein of badly discoloured stone had been left, forming a rough buttress to one side of the uppermost terrace. He dismounted and walked. As he thought, hidden from general view a large but decrepit railway container wagon stood on a foundation of old railway sleepers.

He found Honeypot at his elbow. 'You'd better let me do this,' she said. 'If you're wrong, it could add up to breaking and entering.'

'I'm not wrong. I can hear sounds. And somebody's been here before us – your friend Clive Spicer for sure.' He pointed to the broken timber round the lock.

The door was stiff with rust but between them they managed to slide it open wide enough for a person to pass. The container seemed at first to be full of the paraphernalia of the sport – two clay-pigeon traps, boxes of clays of all colours and sizes, cartridges of all loadings and some variety of bores, impedimenta of all kinds. At first, Michael's heart sank. But he followed a series of small noises and found her. Muriel

Greening had been folded and tied into a ball, knees to chin and ankles to bottom, and a gag was bound into place with many turns of the same blue rope. Her eyes showed only their whites. There was blood in her hair and on her face and she was deeply unconscious, but after a moment during which his heart seemed to hesitate he saw that her breast still rose and fell.

Honeypot stepped back into the sunshine and spoke to Sergeant Grant. 'If she can stand it, we'll take her in my car to meet the ambulance. We may need a stretcher party. I want this quarry securely but secretly watched and guarded for the next twenty-four hours. Somebody may come back for her when they think the heat's off – if Spicer phoned his boss between dropping her off and being caught by the stinger, in which case they haven't had time to get here yet. If not ... it wouldn't exactly break my heart if Spicer were to manage to make a phone call from hospital.'

'Leave it to me, Guv'nor,' said the sergeant.

SIXTEEN

Without quite realizing how it had been stage-managed, they found themselves back at home and quite cut off from all news except for vague, unsubstantiated and inaccurate reports by the media. Attempts to phone Honeypot were frustrated, because her mobile was never switched on except, apparently, when she needed to make calls, and the switchboard at HQ promised to relay messages without ever provoking a reply. While Michael struggled to keep his mind on business, Hilda tried to ask on the hospital network after Muriel Greening's condition, but that name was not overtly recognized by any of Edinburgh's hospitals. Without much hope she began on hospitals scattered through the Lothians. With Clive Spicer she had more luck. It seemed almost that the New Royal Infirmary was anxious to spread the word of his presence (and nothing else) in exchange for finding out the identity of the enquirer. They were sure that they could detect the hand of the police, almost certainly of Honeypot herself, behind the various moves.

Her enquiries eventually bore fruit by, as it were, a back door. After three barren days had passed, DCI Honeypot Laird made an appearance. Michael, when he saw the arrival of the now familiar Range Rover, was ready to make a guess as to her business and attitude from her choice of companion, but she turned out to be alone. This he found surprising. Police officers usually go in a minimum of pairs, for reasons of mutual protection and value of evidence. She seemed tired and dispirited and a little less immaculate than her usual self. Even the Range Rover, usually sparkling, seemed slightly dusty. She accepted a seat in front of the fire and even asked politely for a cup of tea. Evidently all was not well with Honeypot.

'I daren't discuss this with my colleagues,' she said after the minimum of courtesies. She seemed to be addressing a point midway between Hilda and Michael. 'I'm working under the Scottish Crime and Drugs Enforcement Agency and there have been leaks from the rank and file, so I've been warned to keep this confidential under threat of penalties such as you wouldn't believe. On the other hand you have shown that, given good reason, you can keep a secret. But, at the same time, while we're struggling to maintain a screen of secrecy, you've been making enquiries of the hospitals. I dare say that this was only out of concern for Mrs Greening's health but it does constitute a risk to security. The best way to ensure your silence is to tell you what's going on. That leaves you with no reason to run on a parallel track. At the same time I need advice and you used to be a computer consultant. Am I right?'

'True,' Michael said. 'But I may be going a little rusty.'

'We'll see. We have reason to believe that a major fraud is in the making but that's all we know. Names have been mentioned but the owners of those names are either missing or hospitalized or keeping silent. For obvious reasons we would prefer to nip it in the bud before it happens. I can't expect you to produce a solution to the conundrum, but you'll have my gratitude if you can furnish me with a few wise words to say at the next discussion between the big wheels – discussions that I only get dragged to because there's a local connection.'

'You know about hacking?' Michael asked.

Honeypot shrugged. 'I know what the word means. I wouldn't know the first thing about how to do it.'

'Then this may make your big wheels sit up and take notice. When I was a student in computing, a lot of comparatively innocent hacking went on. One group monitored the medical records of senior police officers. They thought that if they ever needed a little help with something like a speeding summons it could be useful to know which senior officers have ever caught the – um – clap, if you'll forgive the expression. I don't know that the information was ever used but you could cause a stir with it. You might even watch to see who changes colour.'

Honeypot pursed her lovely lips in a silent whistle. 'I'll bear your suggestion in mind. It seems to me that our problem is that nothing has happened yet, except for these ripples that you know about; yet the whispers are that this is bigger than Paul Penicuik, bigger even than Alec Jenkinson, and if we let it happen it will already be too late to avert serious consequences. I'll summarize. There's a London gang leader. I've mentioned him before. You wouldn't recognize his real name but the nearest equivalent in English is Mr Sweet, so that's how he's known. He's into everything that's crooked. He's already a billionaire but that doesn't satisfy him. He's a megalomaniac. If it doesn't sound too James Bond, I don't think that world domination would be enough for him. Our informant, now deceased, heard him boasting, in his cups, and passed the word along. That informant is not seen around any more – as you know, he met a remarkably unpleasant fate – so you can see the level of trust that I'm investing in you and asking you to have in me. His boast was that he had got or was about to get his hands on an undetectable system for using the Internet to procure unlimited funds. Alec Jenkinson's name cropped up more than once.

'So we have been watching and listening. Most of the known, possible frauds using the Internet have already been analyzed, explored and watched for, but nothing much is stirring. The hunt has been so thorough that eleven people are now on remand for frauds committed using the Internet, but those are small fry. Either the big one hasn't started yet or it really is new and so subtle that we can't detect it. There seems to have been no unusual movement of money. Any comments so far?'

Michael's imagination had been running ahead. 'I've no specialist knowledge,' he said. 'My first step, usually, would be to rush to the Internet and Google "Fraud", but presumably that's already away in the past. So let's look at it logically. There are ways of hacking in and conjuring money out of somebody else's bank account and into another, but they leave traces behind that can be followed, given time, skill and patience. I can imagine ways of making a small number of transactions untraceable, but the fact that something had happened would always show. Anyway the profit could hardly be described as "unlimited". Other

216

frauds could be carried out from within a company. Why were you interested in the Greenings and Quimbles?'

Honeypot hesitated and then shrugged. 'The same informant caught those names without any context.'

Hilda coughed modestly. 'You've asked Muriel Greening?'

Honey hesitated, looking seriously from one to the other. 'This you must keep totally confidential. Mrs Greening is a very sick woman. It seems that she was unwise enough to resist being kidnapped by Clive Spicer when he caught up with her. Unfortunately he doesn't know his own strength – as a result he will be very unpopular with his employers. He intended no more than to subdue her or knock her unconscious, but she fell and hit her head on a stone step. Mrs Greening suffered a badly fractured skull and is in a coma. Whether she will ever recover from it and, if so, have any memory of events leading up to that injury the doctors can't tell us but they are not optimistic. And it has been Mr Greening's turn to disappear.'

Hilda was shocked into silence. Michael

said, 'From what you've told us so far two words stand out – *undetectable* and *unlimited*. Those rule out any fraud that I've heard of so far. Fraud assumes that money has been removed from somewhere and the fact that it has gone would surely be noticed by somebody. I can only visualize the Internet being the communications medium in a fraud that is not electronic in nature. You follow me?'

Honeypot seemed uncertain but determined not to admit it. Hilda jumped in. 'I do. Look at it this way. Suppose somebody found out all the necessary passwords and ciphers and sent an instruction to – let's say – the Royal Mint to start printing large-denomination notes and to go on until told to stop. That's just an oversimplified example but you see what Mike means?'

For a moment Honeypot seemed to see a great light dawning, but then the sun hid behind a cloud. 'You make it sound easy but in fact it's fenced with difficulties. You might get them to print the notes but how could you collect the money without arousing suspicions or getting caught? You could hardly turn up at a safe deposit with a trainload of bank notes.'

Hilda looked chagrined. 'I was only trying to explain what Mike meant.'

Honeypot patted her hand. 'I'm sorry. I know you were and I get the point.'

'Maybe I can help in a different way,' Hilda said. 'I've heard that when somebody's unconscious they can sometimes still hear voices and the sound of a friendly voice can help them to recover. Muriel Greening seems rather a withdrawn sort of person but we got on well. I think that she might think of me as a friend. I could go and talk to her.'

'I don't think so,' Honeypot said reluctantly. 'I've heard the same thing – in fact I saw it tried once. The patient recovered but whether that was due to the voice or the natural resilience of the human body I wouldn't know. But in this instance the risk of leading hostile forces to her bedside may be too great. I'll consult my superiors but the answer will probably be "Thanks but no thanks". And in the meantime you've no more positive suggestions to offer?'

'I'm afraid not,' said Michael. 'Only that you have to step aside from the usual boundaries and think wider.'

'I came to you,' Honeypot said, 'in the hope that you might be able to help me to do just that. But apparently not.'

However, it was Honey's turn to be wrong. She returned the next day. Her orders, she said, were to convey Hilda personally to visit Muriel Greening in the hospital and to be responsible for her safety. For day after day, five or six days a week, Honey would turn up, usually but not always with the Range Rover, and whisk Hilda in considerable comfort to the chosen hospital. Hilda was returned home at various times of the afternoon or evening suited to Honey's other responsibilities and had to cope with most of the housekeeping as well as the clerical side of Michael's business in whatever time she could win for herself. She noticed that they never followed the same route twice running. Honey explained that using a regular route would turn the follower's job from difficult to very easy.

Muriel Greening, much bandaged, had a cubicle to herself. It was drab and utilitarian but at least the visitor's chair was comfortable. She was guarded by one of three men in turn. The men wore white coats but Hilda soon recognized these as camouflage because each also had a bulge under one armpit and an air of self-sufficiency in any crisis. An individual who tried to visit her by claiming to be her brother was arrested in a manner far from gentle. He turned out to be a reporter on the track of a story. This was about to find its way as a side-bar into his paper, but word reached the police and an embargo was slapped on it. Nobody else tried it.

Muriel lay prone and pale but as time passed the traces of hairdresser, manicurist and beautician under the bandages faded and she could be seen to age at many times the speed ordained by nature. She was anchored by several tubes and wires which were serviced by nursing staff who seemed less than optimistic about the value of their efforts. Opinion, which they never expressed except by unconscious body language, was that but for the insistence of the police, life support would have been withdrawn.

Hilda had liked Muriel but they had not exchanged very many words in the past. Not being friends as such, there were no shared do-you-remembers. It was not long before she found herself running out of topics. From the second day she took in a selection of newspapers to read out and discuss. But somehow that seemed to be missing the personal element that Hilda felt would be fundamental to the unusual therapy. After the first week, however, she began to describe the preparations that were being made for her wedding. It might have been coincidence, but from that point onward the hospital staff claimed to detect a stirring of interest revealed by the trace drawn by the EEG machine.

So the daily monologue began to include progress reports about the wedding plans. One of her bodyguards took quite an interest. Mr Gilmour had insured against the day ever since the birth of his daughter, so where he was concerned the limit, if not sky high, was quite far in that direction. With Hilda's time so largely committed to the patient much of the planning was necessarily left to her delighted mother, with only telephoned consultations allowing Hilda to veto such wild flights as cathedrals, white satin and bridesmaids by the dozen strewing rose petals. The date for the wedding had now settled in December, the last month in which there was a reasonable chance of the bump not being conspicuous enough to offend old-fashioned sensibilities. Hilda had to point out that she did not even know so many potential bridesmaids and that rose petals in December might be in short supply.

In her chats to Muriel Greening, Hilda began to include and even to embellish the details of these discussions of wedding plans with her mother, turning each one into a little anecdote, and she was almost sure that the patient's mouth sometimes showed a trace of a smile. Finding in herself a talent for humorous monologue never before suspected, Hilda was tempted to include the story of Estelle and the revenge that was awaiting her.

It happened that Estelle had bitterly offended both her parents by endeavouring to forbid them, on the grounds of respectability, from attending a play at the local theatre – a play which was considered risqué by those who had elected themselves the guardians of their neighbours' morals. Such was their annoyance at being treated as children by one of their own that Mr and Mrs Gilmour had embraced, with tears of laughter, the concept of the fictitious but disreputable family tree being unveiled by the groom in his wedding speech, with the sole proviso that the guests (other than Estelle and her husband) be warned in confidence and at the last minute that the tale was a fiction.

Hilda was sorely tempted to tell the whole story to the inert figure on the bed but, with one or another bodyguard present and God knew what medical ears liable suddenly to intrude, it was impossible. The joke, if revealed, would be too good not to do the rounds at record speed. She contented herself therefore with explaining that the groom's speech would include a quite hilarious revelation. It might have been her imagination but she was almost sure that Mrs Greening's usually expressionless face registered disappointment, so she finished by saying, 'I'll tell you all about it as soon as I'm back from my honeymoon; or if you can get better in time, of course, you'll certainly be invited to my wedding.'

She thought that the figure on the bed made the sound usually represented as 'Mm?' What is certain is that from that moment Muriel Greening began the long climb towards recovery. No instant leap into total recall was to be expected, but she passed, at a speed that amazed her doctors, from making small sounds of recognition into brief but intelligible conversations about simple matters such as her own comfort, likes and dislikes. Individual personal recollections were still far off – indeed, in the opinion of the psychologist who had been nominated to supervise her mental recovery, she appeared to know more about Hilda's history and circumstances than her own, but at least she was moving in the right direction.

The working area at home was in danger of reverting to the very state that Hilda had first been engaged to rectify, but Hilda was persuaded to continue her hospital visits all the same.

SEVENTEEN

As the date chosen for the wedding came rushing closer, Hilda could not help being sucked into taking part in its planning and preparations. Michael was responsible for most of the pre-planning entailed in preparation for the bridegroom's speech.

The list of guests was still growing. It was soon clear that Muriel Greening, despite her progress, could not possibly be fit to attend, but Honeypot was taking an interest and seemed to be angling for an invitation. Mr Gilmour, once the threats of cathedrals, rose petals and white satin had been removed, had found that his insurance policies were more than enough for the feeding and watering of their friends and neighbours and had been broadcasting invitations. Nearly all of these had been accepted and he made a special case for Honeypot who was not only well known and famously photogenic but was the daughter of one of the kingpins of Scottish finance. Others felt that the presence of a police officer of some seniority might dampen the festivities. The bride, however, had become friendly towards Honey during their travels together and, knowing her friends and neighbours, also felt that the festivities might well be in need of a little dampening. The question remained under review.

Six days before the wedding the guests were allowed to know that a sensational revelation would be made at the wedding. They were also advised that if anybody, even one of participants, were so much as to whisper that fact in their dreams their invitation would be withdrawn. The threat must have been sufficient because three days later there was no whisper on the subject in the town and any mention of the wedding referred only to such matters as the number of invitees, the quantity of drink to be provided and whether the bride was a virgin. This last was the one question that almost everybody answered correctly. Immediately prior to the wedding they would be allowed to know that the revelation would be wholly fictitious.

Estelle and her husband were left strictly in the dark, but two days before the wedding (an interval carefully calculated to allow time for panic but not for research) the report and family tree were sent by email. Again, only a business name was attached. There was a brief period of panic when it was learned through Mrs Gilbertson that Estelle considered herself to be too busy to waste time looking at her emails.

After some head-scratching Estelle was sent an email from Hilda inviting her to be a matron of honour at the wedding. Through the same lady they managed to advise Estelle that she should check her emails. For several hours Hilda almost held her breath but after that time the hoped-for curt refusal arrived.

But before that time there had been big doings.

Four days before the wedding, Honeypot deposited Hilda, as usual, at the gate of her house. A longstanding frost had given way to colourless clouds and a white light; and snow was falling. The snow in the drive was unmarked, which told Hilda that Michael had remained indoors at least for the past few hours. She found him at home and, as if in answer to her prayers, he had made a good start to the packing. This was a major undertaking because Mr Gilmour, in his relief at finding a healthy surplus left from his insurance policies, had decided that his wedding present to the happy couple would be an extravagant honeymoon lasting three weeks. Michael had chosen the hotel at which his unhappy encounter with Estelle had taken place. It had seemed to be a beautiful and well-appointed place but he had not managed to enjoy its facilities on their first visit. The Gilmours had even agreed to keep Russet for the duration; but in view of the season the couple had decided to leave the motorbike and the car at home and to do most of the journey by Orient Express.

A long holiday in Switzerland at Christmas meant that most of their clothes must be taken or sent by carrier, so that careful selection was required. The pair worked through the evening and retired to bed exhausted, but at least the job was done and necessary preparations were made to leave the house secure but safe from frost.

Hilda had got into the habit of sleeping in an old shirt of Michael's, but that would not do for her pre-bridal nights at home and certainly not for her honeymoon abroad. Her exquisite new nightdresses were to be saved for the proper occasions, so she went to bed with a pair of panties as her only nightwear.

It may have been the unfamiliar sensation of sleeping topless. Perhaps she was unsettled by Honeypot's mention of the precautions that were being taken for her safety, which included regular visits by any patrols that found themselves in the area of Spring Cottage and an instruction to an armed-response unit that a call to Michael and Hilda's house was to be treated as a matter of rather more urgency than merely urgent. She was also unsettled by Michael's new habit of taking both his shotgun and a heavy hammer to bed with him, constant reminders that she might well be supposed to be the one person privy to Muriel Greening's secret. Whatever the reason, Hilda had only just dropped into a doze at midnight when Russet nosed her elbow. Her eyes snapped open and, by the moonlight reflecting off the snow and back down from the bedroom ceiling, she saw that the young dog was looking at her anxiously, wanting reassurance. That, Hilda thought, made two of them.

Her eyes told her nothing more. With her fingers twined in Russet's coat, she listened and heard a clack that she had heard a thousand times before. It was the sound of the front door lock.

Hilda had never been the sort of girl to scream and clutch at the nearest man; nor was fleeing part of her repertoire. She slipped out of bed, tiptoed to the bedroom door and eased it open for a peep outside. The hall was flooded with light. It should have been dark and it was cold when it should have been warm. The door was standing open. Her sleep-fuddled mind refused to recognize danger until a black figure loomed in front of her.

The intruder was given confidence by the sawn-off shotgun that he carried. His confidence might have been dented if he had known that Hilda, at her boarding school, had been taught self-defence by a lesbian gym teacher who regarded all men as guilty until proved innocent (which never happened) and their appendages as adjuncts that they were much better without. Hilda also recalled the effect on Brian Foley of the blow delivered by Michael. Luckily for the intruder she did not have a knife to hand. She made an instinctive grab for the gun and would probably have been blown in half if the gun had not been one of very high value before it was sawn off; its perfect mechanism had automatically applied the safety catch when the gun was opened for loading. At the same moment she executed a quick kick to the testes, exactly as taught. The man dropped to his knees in agony, and his breath eventually returned, first as a whistle, then as a groan and finally as a fully fledged wail that continued after Hilda was sure that he must have run out of breath. He had released his grip on the sawn-off gun.

The second intruder, who had been detailed to follow the first inside as a back-up, had been born and raised in Haiti. He was intensely superstitious and the blackness of the shadows lent strength to an already overactive imagination. The sudden appearance, apparently out of nowhere, of a pale and seemingly naked goddess who first disarmed his leader and then smote him down, was too much. He turned and fled through the doorway, crying out words of warning in a language that nobody present could understand and throwing away as he went a cheap, Belgian-made semi-automatic pistol.

Hilda's blood was thoroughly up. She set off in pursuit. Being woken at midnight in her own home and threatened with a sawn-off shotgun was enough, she felt, to annoy anyone. Moreover Russet, barking with excitement, had joined in the chase and received a kick that made her yelp. Hilda's anger turned to fury.

Two men were waiting outside. The sudden appearance of a near-naked girl in the falling snow was so improbable as to disorient their thinking, but it was also obvious that she was waving around a sawn-off shotgun in a manner that could only be considered highly dangerous. One man was armed with a muzzle-loading revolver, made in a back street of Islamabad and brought back to the UK as a souvenir, or so Honey was later assured by an expert of her acquaintance. That man fired one shot that hit nothing and then hurried to get behind a tree.

His movement distracted Hilda, who turned to follow it. This gave the fourth man his chance. He darted round Hilda, seized her from behind and grabbed the gun. Her movements were such that he caught the gun by the muzzle. Her grip on the stock had also resulted in the safety catch being snicked off. His jerk at the muzzle caused the gun to fire, taking off the tip of his finger. Shock can delay the beginning of pain whereas excitement can be instant and so it was some seconds before the man realized that the fun of grasping a struggling girl clad only in panties was eclipsed by the pain where his fingertip had formerly been. His immediate impulse – to release her in order to nurse his wound – was negated by the fact that her struggles were violent and her intention was clearly to do him some serious injury with her teeth or fingernails. It was, in fact, the classic case of having the proverbial tiger by the tail. The shotgun had already fallen barrel-first into the snow and, whether the participants knew it or not, would almost certainly have burst if the other barrel had been fired. Fortunately it had become lost for the moment in the snow.

If the antagonists had been left to themselves the stalemate could have lasted indefinitely. Russet circled them, barking furiously.

The first arrival was Michael, who had paused to put on some clothes and shoes before loading his own shotgun and hurrying out to the rescue. That he had done so in considerable haste was proved by the fact that some of the clothes were Hilda's. The man who had originally been the first intruder was beginning to recover the power of movement and got a clip with the hammer behind his right ear for his pains.

Now that the sawn-off shotgun was under snow the man behind the tree had recovered his nerve and was hurrying to join the fun. There was a quick way to stop that and Michael took it. He fired a one-handed shot from the hip over the heads of the three people in the open. Even out of doors, the

235

slam of a twelve-bore magnum cartridge loaded for geese was mind-numbing and the vibration shook snow from the overhead branches in a dozen places. Hilda found herself free for the moment but before she could begin her programme of reprisals Michael had her by the arm and swung her round. 'Go and put some clothes on,' he said.

Hilda began to come out of her berserk frenzy. She realized for the first time that she was very exposed and very, very cold. Adrenaline vanished as though the chain had been pulled. She bolted for the house.

Michael reloaded the one barrel that he had fired and prepared to sell his life dearly for Hilda's sake but that sacrifice proved unnecessary. A bright light, almost blinding in the snow, lit the whole scene and an amplified voice, only slightly muffled by the snow, announced that armed police had arrived and invited those present to drop their guns or be shot.

Michael had saved for two years to afford that shotgun and he was not going to drop it in the snow for anybody. He did however place it carefully on the log pile and back away, raising his hands a token amount and then, when he remembered that police in Britain are no longer as protective of innocent bystanders as once they were, as high as they could go. The visitors also heeded the warning except for one man who was dancing around in a circle, spraying blood from his fingertip. He was judged not to be a threat and his life was spared.

Less than an hour later, Honey had arrived. They gathered that she had been fetched from her bed but she was as neat as a pin. She apologized for the late arrival of the rescuers but pointed out that this was not Los Angeles or New York and that it took time to alert and move an armed-response unit.

'I thought that they were phenomenally quick,' Michael said.

'I wish I could agree. They might not have arrived at all except that a beat bobby in Edinburgh saw four men being met by a hired car driven by a local hoodlum who he recognized – the one who later lost a fingertip. The bobby happened to be that rarity, a man who reads and remembers all the circulars. He recognized the men from their descriptions and raised the alarm.'

Hilda, who was now fully dressed and also wrapped in a duvet, was frowning. 'We only saw four men,' she said. 'But what you just told us adds up to five.'

'The big boss was waiting in the car,' Honey explained. 'Not the biggest of the lot, but Alec Jenkinson. I think he wanted to question you without any delay. We found some cord in his pocket, a pair of pliers and several lighters.'

There was a long pause while her words were assimilated and imaginations got to work. 'That's awful,' Hilda whispered. Her teeth had stopped chattering as she warmed up but, as the implication of what had awaited her sank in, the rhythmic drumming began again.

'It's an acceptable result,' Honey said cheerfully. 'We can show that they all travelled together and that four out of the five arrived here armed and ready to commit violence. That should be enough for a court to tuck them away while we complete our enquiries. With a bit of luck we should be able to find out what they're after before the lawyers manage to get them out.'

'And if you don't?' Michael asked.

Honey shrugged. She stretched out her hands to the fire. Dawn was almost due. 'Better luck next time,' she said. 'Of course, the man we really want is the big boss in London, Mr Sweet.' Her eyes glowed with the fervour of one who sees the Holy Grail. 'If we can find evidence to put him away they'll put up a statue of me outside Scotland Yard in place of that rather odd triangular sign. They do not like their prize informants being murdered. It tends to discourage the others.' She got to her feet. 'I think we can all sleep soundly now, at least for a few days.'

Hilda said, 'I'm not sure that I'll ever sleep again.'

'I go along with that,' said Michael.

Honey laughed merrily. 'Nonsense,' she said briskly. 'Just remember that anybody likely to wish you harm will be locked away, with the police, meaning yours truly, vigorously opposing bail. And if, due to some freakish insanity on the part of the justiciary, bail is granted, you will already be abroad on your honeymoon and I will personally explain to each one of them that their interest in you has been noted and that any moves in your direction, unfriendly or otherwise, will result in another and even quicker trip back to the slammer, with a blind eye being turned to any reluctance to resist arrest.'

Hilda and Michael returned to bed. Whether due to this assurance or to exhaustion, they slept very well. They awoke simultaneously in the morning, and Michael found Hilda eyeing him anxiously. He yawned and stretched. 'Promise me two things,' he said. 'If such an emergency should ever happen again ... One, you will wait until I'm ready to back you up before you go off pop. And, two, you will pause and put some clothes on. When we're married, I shall not feel like sharing your naked loveliness with every passing assailant; nor will I want any police officers bent on rescuing us to be distracted.'

Hilda blushed scarlet.

EIGHTEEN

Their penultimate day as an unmarried couple dawned white with a dark but colourless sky. Snow, now almost knee-deep, still lay white as a swan's down on land and roofs and treetops so that walls and upright surfaces stood out, black and uncompromising. The breeze had dropped away.

The excitement from their midnight visitors was fading but not forgotten. Each was inclined to jump at sudden noises or unexpected shadows.

The radio was suggesting that only the most necessary journeys be undertaken. Over breakfast, Hilda and Michael agreed that their marriage would not have been a matter of necessity except that Hilda's father had already committed himself to heavy expenditure that would not be covered by his insurance if the wedding did not take place. Honeypot had accepted her invitation to the wedding but regretfully was unable to provide transport. And so, with misgivings, they packed the car, added Russet's bed on top of the cases, took the setter at the passenger's feet, topped up the car's screenwash bottles, locked the house and set off. They loved their home but it was no longer their impregnable castle. They felt safer away from the scene of so much violence. Locking the house was no simple matter, however. The expensive digital lock had been removed by crowbar, producing the sound that had alarmed Russet, and it had to be repaired and refixed. The old-fashioned mortise lock had been picked in the conventional manner.

The snowfall had reduced to occasional and local flurries and, even where the ploughs and gritting lorries had not yet returned since the last heavy fall, warm tyres had turned most of the roads into slushy rivers across the virgin white. Where the tyres could dig down to the road's surface Hilda managed well, but Michael had more experience of driving on slippery surfaces, so wherever the rear wheels showed a desire to overtake the front he took over. Just once, his skill proved insufficient and he terrified them both by doing an unintentional three-hundred-and-sixty-degree twirl. Fortunately they met little other traffic.

The Gilmour family home, though built to Victorian standards, was too small to accommodate the wedding guests and although there was a lawn large enough to hold a marquee it was not the season for going under canvas. Moreover, Hilda and Michael were agreed that organized religion was for the superstitious and so they had no desire for a religious service. One of the plusher local hotels had been booked for the ceremony and the festivities to follow; rooms had been reserved for guests staying overnight, and the services of a registrar were also reserved. Michael drew in under the porte cochère in the late afternoon. To satisfy superstition rather than propriety, he was to spend two nights there while Hilda returned to her old home. They dined together that evening, with snow falling outside again. Michael put on the Wellingtons that seemed destined to become an important part of his wedding rig, drove her home and then walked back, slithering.

The snow stopped but there was no sign of a thaw. Michael greeted his wedding morning with relief – not on account of the weather but because the intervening wedding eve had been so intolerably boring. Hilda had been too involved in preparations for her wedding to spare attention for her bridegroom. Much of that day he had spent looking out at the snow while his mind turned over and over the possibilities of the Internet for fraud. What areas for chicanery remained unexplored? It was not immediately obvious, but he knew that the answer was there, somewhere just out of reach.

The preparations for the wedding itself seemed to be running forward on oiled wheels but roads were still bad and his own friends were slow to arrive. That evening, his supposed stag party began with Michael present plus two guests; these were a tongue-tied former flatmate from Dundee and the best man – a cousin of Michael by the name of Johnson McRae. Other guests drifted in, late and tired, and the evening proved less than riotous. Michael was not given to over-indulgence, but on this occasion a slightly more bibulous evening would have been welcomed.

On the wedding day, however, everything seemed to race forward like a bolting horse. The service provider proved incapable of screening the calls to his mobile so that, among the calls wishing him well or warning of late arrivals due to local snowfalls, were some from clients who were quite sure that the wife of some remote ancestor had come from this family rather than that or that a grandfather's uncle who had lived his life in some inconspicuous hole in the backwoods had actually been born in some other non-place half a mile further from civilization, and each was prepared to debate the point endlessly. He managed to grab breakfast of a sort but he was trying to dress for his wedding while assuring a client that he was not heir to a dukedom when he discovered that he had left home with a single cuff-link. The hotel manager, who had seen it all before, was able to help out, calm him down and feed him a large brandy. Apart from a tendency to bite his tongue Michael had a grip on himself.

Suddenly, people were thronging into the ballroom where the marriage was to take place. Johnson made sure that Michael was clean and tidy with his carnation in place and his flies fastened and they took their places. Hilda and her bridesmaid made an entrance and the ceremony proceeded to plan – the basic and unadulterated legal requirement with no added vows.

Hilda and Michael exchanged kisses and handshakes with the guests in the doorway between the ballroom and the entrance hall, where the guests were to enjoy drinks of their choice while the bridal couple were led away to be photographed and the ballroom was readied for the evening's celebrations. During this interval Estelle moved among the guests, damning with very faint praise and dripping venom from every orifice. There could be no doubt that she had read the fateful email, but though defiance was added to the underlying arrogance there was no lessening of the hostility. The marriage, she suggested, had not come a moment too soon. Her assertion that hers had always been a respectable family was repeated – and remembered. She would be reminded of it frequently during the coming weeks.

Just when the guests were about to faint from hunger they were marshalled into the dining room. A good meal was served, washed down with generous quantities of wine. By the time for the speeches the guests were in a fine and festive mood and when the groom was called on to speak he was greeted with a chorus of friendly voices.

Michael began by thanking everyone for their contributions to the great day. He went on to say a few words in praise of his lovely bride. He then mentioned the bride's family and at that point Estelle suddenly sat up and her eyes narrowed. Her neighbours at the table swore later that she farted slightly.

'As most of you know,' Michael said, 'I am a genealogist by profession and I have had occasion to do some work on the family into which I have had the privilege of marrying. My bride's antecedents may be of some interest to you all.'

Estelle, very white about the nose and ears but red everywhere else, got to her feet and made for the nearest doorway. She might have been seeking a toilet but few of the guests were fooled. She found the door closed and locked. So too, by arrangement with the hotel staff, were the other doors. Her husband, who, if not proved innocent of complicity in the accusing email had never been proved guilty, had been taken aside a few minutes earlier and escorted willingly from the room. A hush fell as one and all realized that the promised revelation was imminent.

'The major branch of the Gilmours' family tree,' Michael resumed, 'begins with Captain Goldbender of Granton, who commanded the trading ship *Stella*, sailing out of Leith during the eighteenth century. It was in her honour that the name Stella, sometimes modified to Estelle, has been preserved in the family.'

Estelle beat on one of the doors with her fists. 'Open this damn door!' she cried. Anyone but Estelle would have seen that she was being victimized in an elaborate hoax but having been born without the least trace of a sense of humour she was unable to recognize humour in others. Nobody paid any attention.

'In 1763 the captain sailed for Bordeaux

to fetch a cargo of wine. They were to rendezvous with a dozen fishing boats in the vicinity of the Bell Rock, to avoid the payment of duty. He took with him his lady friend, Hermione Batley, for what was intended, as far as they were concerned, purely as a pleasure trip. Miss – or Mrs as it later transpired – Batley had had a somewhat chequered past, but this we can ignore.

'The ship's log, which is more detailed than was the custom, can still be inspected in the muniments room of the Merchant Navy Society. It seems that before they had even reached Bordeaux there had been a falling-out and Ms Batley, as we may as well continue referring to her, transferred her affections to the first mate, one Hector Pringle. The captain married them, as he was empowered to do, and no mention was made of the fact that each already had a spouse back in Scotland.

'While the wine was being loaded, the captain had word of another and far more lucrative cargo to be had at Marseilles. The cargo, it turned out, consisted of young women destined for what was known as the "white slave trade", along with their escorts. It must have been an uncomfortably crowded journey.'

Estelle showed signs of becoming violent. The bridesmaid and one of Hilda's cousins, previously primed for the job, steered her gently to a chair and then each held one of her hands so that she could not put her fingers in her ears.

'The *Stella* sailed to Buenos Aires. The passengers were to complete their journeys overland. The cargo of wine was disposed of profitably and Captain Goldbender found that the South American ports offered a variety of valuable cargoes without any need to share the profit with the ship's real owners. It seems to have been a happy as well as a lucrative voyage which extended to several years, during which time Ms Batley, who was of a quarrelsome nature, had been passed from one to another of the crew. The ship returned to Britain and eventually to Leith, by which time she had given birth to three children, a boy and two girls. The paternity of those children was in some doubt, and because the marital status of the most probable fathers was unclear it had been decided to register each birth using as a surname the next port of call.

'They must have been mad to make a return visit to Leith. It did not last long. The ship's owners, the owners of the original cargo of wine, the excisemen and various spouses were all on the warpath. Betty Santos, Mary Montevideo and the unfortunately named William Florianopolis were left in Fife with relatives of what were hoped to be the correct members of the crew. An attempt was made to leave again on a night of darkness and fog but the ship suffered an unfortunate collision with the Bass Rock and was lost. The few survivors from the crew were imprisoned but no sign of the captain was seen again.

'That might have been an end to the matter except that, nearly two decades later, William and Betty met at a barn dance. Quite unaware that they were half-siblings, they fell in love, but Betty declared that she had suffered long enough with the outlandish name of Santos and that no way was she changing it for the worse to Florianopolis. And so William took the name of his employer, Gilmour. They were blessed with a son who later married a Helena Montevideo.'

Michael paused for his glass to be refilled. The company had sat in silence, determined not to miss a word of the tangled tale of incest. Now, as they recognized the name, there was a buzz of interest and they released their suppressed amusement in a clap of laughter. Hotel staff used the break to go round again with the wine bottles. Estelle had lowered her head and was trying to escape public attention by burrowing under the tablecloth. Honeypot, who had tried to laugh while taking a mouthful of red wine, had to be wiped with napkins.

When Michael spoke again there was immediate silence. The details that he gave need not be repeated. A pedantically minded listener might have noticed certain conflicts of dates but there were no nit-pickers present that day. He managed to weave in the names of Burke and Hare, several infamous rapists, a witch who had been burned at the stake ... the list went on. Near his conclusion he introduced a character named Aunt Edith who had tried hard to incriminate her own sister and her future brother-in-law on a charge of cannibalism. The word picture that he painted of Aunt Edith was easily recognized as Estelle. He finished with a reference to Lucrezia Borgia, which would have been quite enough to assure any listener of the fictitious nature of his revelations (if such were needed in view of the helpless laughter of the bride's parents). Estelle, however, was beyond recognizing such details. She was led out of the room and left to release her nerve storm and compose herself in a bedroom, with the bridesmaid in attendance. The humour had passed her by but the implications had not.

The happy couple was not due to fly out to the honeymoon destination until the afternoon of the following day and so they were able to stay for the evening's festivities. It was understood that Estelle had a migraine and would not be coming down to join in. Hilda danced until her feet hurt but Michael, after the unavoidable duty dances were behind him, spent much of his time in the bar, trying hard to avoid the excessive glasses of whisky that were thrust at him. More than one of these arrived in the hand of his father-in-law, who also brought relatives to introduce in the manner of a conjuror producing rabbits from a hat. The only one of these that Michael could recall later was a thin, elderly man with receding grey hair, a darker moustache, popping eyes and unnaturally white teeth. Mr Gilmour introduced him as his cousin, Julius Feeley, and explained that Julius was a stockbroker. From the slightly patronizing manner of the introduction Michael gathered that stockbrokers did not come top in the pecking order when men of finance were gathered together.

While they chatted about the weather, the hotel's décor and weddings generally, Michael's mind was running on quite another tack. The answer that he had been seeking was drifting towards the surface. 'Dealings on the stock market must depend heavily on computers,' he suggested.

'You'd better believe it,' said the other man. 'Those of us who didn't grow up with them have had to learn the hard way. That's me. Cyberprat dot com.'

'I'm not thinking of emails,' Michael said. His thoughts came together with an almost audible click. 'The value of stocks varies according to the trading that's been going on in them, right?'

'True.'

'Most of those deals would be made and confirmed by some variant of email?'

'True.'

Michael was still feeling his way. 'And those dealings have to be recorded, brought together and coordinated into assessments of value for purposes of the next lot of deals. I'm certainly not planning anything, but is there any central point in the system where a dedicated hacker could break in and manipulate the flow of information to his own advantage?'

Julius's sandy eyebrows went up. 'Causing a rise or fall of a particular stock? That isn't how it works.'

Michael's spirits fell. 'Ah well,' he said, 'the question was worth asking.'

'No,' said Julius, 'you'd have to have four very secret email addresses and then crack a code.'

Michael was struggling to find his way through a fog of alcohol. 'But that code itself would have to be embedded in a computer program that could be hacked into?'

'I suppose so.'

'So a brilliant hacker, given a little luck, could break into the system and make his shares in, say, ICI go through the roof?'

Julius was looking worried. 'Not ICI, no. Ford, perhaps. You didn't get any of this from me, remember.'

'Of course not.' Shifting position slightly, Michael was able to see between the dancers. Honeypot was coming off the floor, arm in arm with a sandy-haired man who had been introduced as her husband. In response to Michael's signals the couple altered course and joined him, but he was thwarted in his intention by his father-in-law who reappeared, like a genie from a trap, to make sure that nobody went thirsty. When satisfied on this point and spotting another guest with an empty glass he vanished again.

'This is Detective Chief Inspector Laird,' Michael said, 'and her husband, Detective Superintendent Laird. So you'll see that any information is falling into properly authorized hands. This is Julius Feeley. He's a stockbroker. I was asking him whether a skilled hacker could manipulate a stock value to his own advantage. It does seem that it would be so difficult that it may not have been considered, but the husband of the injured lady is, I'm told, a very highly skilled hacker.'

'One moment,' said Honeypot. She changed in an instant from a popular and much admired wedding guest into a sharp-eyed officer. The faint glow that champagne and bonhomie can convey vanished like the morning dew. She turned to her husband. 'This may not be for your ears,' she said.

'But—'

'I know that you are my senior, but in this matter I am responsible to Crime and Drugs and I was warned, very firmly, that all information is on a need-to-know basis.'

'But these—'

'These people are witnesses and they are giving me information. I hope,' she added.

The detective superintendent turned away, muttering to himself. Michael took him by the elbow. 'I suspect that we're both *de trop* for the moment. Let me get you a drink.'

Honeypot had already relieved her husband of his favourite pen and was busily making notes on the back of a bar menu. 'Tell me exactly how a hacker might go about it,' she said.

NINETEEN

The Orient Express proved to be as luxurious as its reputation promised, and, though rather old-fashioned in its amenities, the depth of winter made up for the lack of air-conditioning. It carried them across most of Europe in considerable comfort and at great expense. A local train and then a hired car conveyed them to their hotel.

In stricter times, a honeymoon was a period set aside for a newly married couple to get over the shock of intimacy and to make all the adjustments that may become necessary. Nowadays, the justification for such an expensive holiday may be less clear-cut. Marriage may be regarded as having no more function than to provide legal protection for the woman and children, in which case the honeymoon is only conformity to an established pattern.

Hilda and Michael had been cohabiting happily for a year and a half. The only shock that they had to overcome was that of losing the spice of the forbidden. The act of physical love had passed from expressing trust by means of an exciting defiance of ancient codes to being an expression of affection combined with a sensory demand. There was a break for several nights while they reappraised their attitudes. Each was hurt to find the other no longer eager to copulate. When their first hesitation was over, nature reasserted itself and they were lovers again, happy with it.

The hotel was as beautiful and comfortable as ever and this time Michael was able to appreciate its qualities to the full. The cuisine was excellent. The hotel was not set very high so that the snow was not yet deep – indeed they had experienced deeper snow on their wedding day – but the views over the frozen lake to the snow-clad Alps were superb. The staff, however, at first showed a reserve that was later explained when the head waiter, an Italian, drew Michael aside for a fatherly word. Begging forgiveness he spoke frankly. The pair had been recognized as the couple who had stayed there earlier in the year. Part of the fracas with Estelle had been seen by a junior chef cooling off in the shadows, and Estelle had again been mistaken for Hilda. The head waiter explained, with tactful circumlocution, that if the lady had so much resented the friendly gesture he could not be doing it correctly. There was a certain tradition ... The head waiter seemed to be on the point of summoning one of the waitresses in order to demonstrate the proper technique when Michael was driven to explain that the caress had been intended for his own lady but in the dim light had been bestowed by mistake on her sister. This explanation circulated immediately among the hotel staff and the pair received smiling service for the remainder of their stay. The younger waitresses giggled at him and scurried past.

The skiing was not yet at its best but Hilda had never been more than a novice skier, and felt she should abstain from such potentially dangerous pursuits given her increasingly obvious pregnancy. Michael was slightly more practised in the sport, and after he visited the lower slopes with hired skis, had a few tumbles and suffered a sprained ankle, they decided that there were other ways to keep themselves entertained.

About halfway through their stay Michael's ankle was still heavily bandaged but he could walk as far as the village with the aid of a pair of sticks. The two were enjoying a drink and a snack in a café in the village when a man in clothing of obviously British cut and style turned a vacant chair from an adjacent table. 'May I join you?' he asked, removing his hat.

It took a second or two for the slightly misshapen nose to cause the pennies to drop. 'Mr Greening,' they said in unison. 'Some people,' Michael went on carefully, 'have been wondering where you were.'

Greening half-smiled. 'I bet,' he said softly. 'It seemed best to get myself well out of the way. I think you'll know what I mean if I say that nobody has any reason to hurt Muriel if they can't use it to put pressure on me.' He looked haggard with stress.

'We understand,' Michael said.

'I've been staying with an old friend in Geneva and another friend back in Scotland has been keeping me posted. He can't find out how Muriel is but he thought that you might know, so when he heard that you were honeymooning here he phoned me and I came straight over. Congratulations, by the way.' He gave a small chuckle but then the look of anxiety returned. 'Passports are no problem. When you've been doing business with both Arabs and Israelis you need to have more than one. So, what can you tell me?'

'How much do you know?' Michael asked.

'I know that she was attacked but not fatally. That was when it seemed better that I get out of sight. As long as I was accessible she could be used to put pressure on me. Her life might even have been threatened.'

Michael glanced around but nobody was paying any attention and their voices were swamped by the babble in the café. 'You were probably right,' he said. 'I'll spell it out for you. Your wife was attacked as part of a kidnap attempt that went wrong. She was injured more seriously than was intended. She was in a coma but she's recovering now. My wife has been going in to sit with her most days on the theory that a friendly voice can aid recovery.'

'It seemed to be working,' Hilda said, 'but her short-term memory was slow to come back. The last that I heard, she still didn't recall anything about your troubles.'

Greening relaxed a little. 'That's good. That she's recovering I mean. It was only for her sake that I got involved at all. And it was good of you to help her.'

Michael had been given time to organize his thoughts. 'The police have been keeping her guarded and isolated. Two weeks ago there was an attack on us at our home. Presumably the intention would have been to force us to tell them her whereabouts. Or there may have been a plan to use us as hostages or to get access to her using us. The police arrived in time and the attackers were captured. Whether or not they're still in custody I don't know.'

'Could you find out? I need to know whether I'm still in danger, or a danger to Muriel.'

Michael weighed the question. 'I expect so,' he said at last.

Greening produced a mobile phone but tapped it uncertainly against the palm of his hand. 'Can we go back to your hotel, do you

264

think? There are too many ears around us.'

Michael and Hilda exchanged a glance. They got to their feet. They had to walk in single file. The short distance back to the hotel was covered in silence except for the clicking of Michael's sticks. It struck Michael as incongruous that the scene of snow, yellow lights and silhouetted buildings, looking as though it belonged on a calendar or in a romantic comedy film, should be the background to such a serious little procession.

They took Greening up to their room. He refused offers of refreshment and kept his sheepskin coat on. Hilda and Mr Greening took the two chairs while Michael reclined on the bed, Roman-emperor style, to ease his ankle.

'My problem,' Greening said, 'is that I don't know whether to cooperate with the police or to hide from them. Are they interested in me as a victim or a suspect? Do you have any idea?'

'You would have to ask DCI Laird,' Hilda said.

'You must have an opinion.'

'If we have,' said Michael, 'it's an opinion

based on an incomplete knowledge of the facts. We've never heard your side of the story. How did you get drawn into it? Tell us that much and we'll give you an opinion if we can reach one.' Hilda gave him an approving glance. She had been wondering how to lead up to the same suggestion.

'It was all very simple and very stupid,' Greening said. 'I was down in London at a conference about electronic security. You know about my interest—'

'In hacking,' Michael finished for him. 'Yes. So do the police.'

'I thought they would, by now. It's been an innocent, academic interest until recently, but, because I've done some research in the area and written one or two articles, I was invited to the conference as a speaker. When I'd given an outline of measures and counter-measures I still had a few minutes of my allotted time in hand so I mentioned that I could see one area in which there was little protection and a huge potential for chicanery.'

'This would be the stock exchange?' Michael suggested.

Greening sighed. 'They've got that far,

have they? I suppose it was inevitable. I had a complete working program prepared, just as a matter of my own interest and with no intention of anyone ever using it.

'Some of the delegates were staying at the same hotel and a session developed in the bar after dinner. I had far too much to drink and I said more than was wise on the subject. I don't know how word got to the man behind it all, but about a week later I was approached by Paul Penicuik. You know him?'

'The local bookie,' Hilda said.

'Exactly. But he was acting for somebody else. First he offered to buy the whole plan or to hire me to carry it out. As soon as I refused he produced some IOUs signed by Muriel. She'd been having a flutter on the horses but I didn't mind that. She'd lost rather more than she'd admitted to me, but what wife wouldn't understate her losses? Her IOUs had been tampered with by a skilled forger...'

Michael swung his feet down to the floor and grunted as his damaged ankle took the shock. 'A forger who was later murdered for talking to the police,' he said. It was all coming together.

Greening lost his colour. 'I didn't know that. But I could believe it. These were the sort of men who believe they're above the law. I could see that Muriel was in the most danger. You were out here at the time so I settled her in your attic and told her to lie low. Soon I was visited by the man I took to be the boss, a fat man with an Eastern European accent, Polish or Lithuanian or something. He was very expensively dress-ed, a good suit and tie with gold links and tiepin, but he sweated a lot. He was accom-panied by a hoodlum who seemed afraid of him.'

'A tall man with a bald head?' Hilda asked.

'That's right.' Greening pursed his lips in a silent whistle. 'My God! You've been mix-ing with some tough company. He addres-sed the fat man as Mr Sweet, if that's any use. They came to my house and I got a punch in the guts straight away.'

'Hurts, doesn't it?' Michael said.

'Does it bloody not! That was just for openers. They didn't make a lot of noise; I suppose they didn't want the neighbours joining in. Mr Sweet made it clear that if I didn't cooperate they would hurt Muriel and I said that they couldn't if they couldn't get at her, which earned me another punch in the belly. The upshot was that I wrote them out a version of my method but I tampered with it, so a fat lot of good it'll do them. They wanted me to demonstrate it to them but as luck would have it I keep my own laptop mostly in the office and only bring it home if I'm expecting to use it. I told them that it was away being repaired. They must have thought that I was quite sufficiently intimidated because they accepted that. They said that they'd be back if it didn't work. That seemed to make it a good time to get out of harm's way so I squared it with my boss, had a word with Muriel and beat it over here. Muriel wouldn't come with me. She has an absolute phobia about foreign countries, for some reason.'

TWENTY

There was silence. Greening dropped the phone, got up and walked to the window. Daylight had faded into a pink glow that lay gently over the snow. Pinpoints of light showed in the valleys. He tugged on the cord that closed the curtains. The bedroom was a precise mirror image of the room that they had occupied on their previous visit.

'It seems to me,' Michael said at last, 'that if you can put your version of the story across you're in the clear. If not, then you've got a real problem. In your shoes I would trust me to phone DCI Laird and ask what the present position is. It's then up to you to consider who may still be a danger to you. Your problem is that the police then have to decide whether your position is as you stated. They may consider a different scenario – that you dreamed up this concept, couldn't

270

manage it unaided and sought help from Penicuik or Sweet. There was a falling-out and the rest happened as you said.'

Greening seemed to be dumbstruck for a second. Then he laughed. 'Why would I need their help?'

'I'm not saying that this happened,' Michael said. 'I'm suggesting that this is what the police might think. It seems to me that you would have the ability to introduce false information into the Stock Exchange system and force the prices of certain stocks either up or down. You wouldn't need help for that. But in order to cash in you would have to make some big purchases and sales and you could only count on it working once. I don't see that an individual without big funds or good credit could ring up one or more stockbrokers and say, "Buy me a million shares of Imperial Chemicals". Or, of course, "Sell ditto on my behalf." If stocks moved the wrong way the broker could find himself stuck with the loss. You'd need somebody with a lot of money or an organization to start off with. If you'd heard whispers that Penicuik wasn't quite straight you might well have approached him. He would then have wanted the weight of somebody bigger behind him. Who would he think of but Alec Jenkinson? But the bigger the operator the more profitable and easier the scam would be. On the principle of little fleas and bigger fleas, he'd turn to Mr Sweet. That's what they might think.'

The silence stretched out longer this time and when Greening spoke there was a slight tremor in his voice. 'You make it sound very convincing. I see that I may not have been very wise to come away like this. I should definitely have a word with your Inspector Laird and exchange our news.'

'I think you'd be sensible. I didn't bring a mobile with me. Lend me yours and I'll get Inspector Laird for you.' Michael looked at his watch. 'She should still be in her office.' He held out his hand.

Greening produced his mobile phone but retained his grip on it. 'Tell me the number. I'll do my own talking.'

'You'll carry more conviction if I introduce you and say that you want to stay on the right side of the law.' He reached out but Greening again held the phone out of reach.

'I don't want her to know where I am until

I can be reasonably sure that I'm in the clear.'

Michael saw Hilda's eyes open wide, behind Greening's shoulder. The ominous implication in his words had not passed her by.

'I can understand that,' Michael said. Greening keyed while Michael quoted the Edinburgh number from memory and then Honeypot's extension number. After a few bleeps of the ringing tone Honeypot's voice answered.

Greening's voice was quite steady. 'This is Frank Greening. I'm calling from somewhere on the continent. No, I don't think that I should say where until my position is a little clearer. First of all, would you please tell me how my wife is recovering?'

The treble glazing and the snow outside combined to muffle all sound so that the room was totally silent. When Honey spoke again her every word could be heard throughout the room. 'Your wife is recovering well from a serious skull fracture. Her memory is still patchy. She is anxious about you.'

'You may tell her that I'm perfectly all right,' Greening said. 'Do you suspect me of complicity in whatever criminal activities have been going on at home?'

There was a pause while Honeypot considered her reply. 'We don't have enough information yet to answer that question,' she said at last. 'Why don't you come and talk to us about it?'

Greening gave a bark of laughter. 'No, thank you very much. You can ask your questions over the phone, now.'

'Very well. But you'll understand that any statements made over the telephone in these circumstances may be recorded but will not carry the same conviction as statements made face to face in front of witnesses.'

'I appreciate that. But would you then tell me, also on the record, whether you think me a member of the gang or an innocent dupe?'

'I would certainly do that when I have enough information. But that would only be my opinion. The opinions that would count would be those of the procurator-fiscal and possibly a judge and a jury.'

'I understand that. All right,' said Greening. 'Ask your questions.'

'Mr Greening, how did your part in or

your connection with this conspiracy begin?'

'You probably know most of this. I had the idea. Stupidly, in my cups, I talked about it. Somebody must have passed the word to Mr Sweet. He would have recruited his Scottish contacts. The first I knew of anybody taking my idea from an academic theory into a practical proposition was about two weeks later. I was approached by Penicuik. I had quite forgotten shooting my mouth off, so I was stunned to find that anyone knew about my idle thoughts. He first invited me to join the club, as you might say; then he began to put pressure on me. He threatened my wife so I tucked her out of harm's way, as I thought. Somehow, he must have found her.' Michael and Hilda exchanged a guilty look. 'You know more than I do about what became of her. Then he began threatening me. That seemed to be a good time to fade out of sight.'

'I can see how it might,' said Honeypot's voice. 'Did you know that Mr and Mrs McGinnis were the subject of a midnight attack three weeks ago?'

'I had heard something of it. I trust that

neither of them was hurt.' Greening winked at Michael, who had the presence of mind to reply in kind.

'No, luckily,' said Honeypot. 'Five men were roped in by an armed response unit. Shots had been fired and there was clear evidence of intent to kidnap. The present assumption is that Mrs McGinnis – Miss Gilmour she was at that time – was the target and the intention would have been to force her to reveal your wife's whereabouts. Three of the men have cooperated, trading their statements against promises that those statements would be mentioned in court as militating in their favour. Two had only peripheral knowledge but one man was close to Mr Sweet. He had more to lose than the others because he was the one who had injured your wife and later had fired a shot. His statement agreed totally with such facts as we already knew, but he added that you brought the proposition to Penicuik in the first place who then took it to Jenkinson who in turn brought in Mr Sweet. He states that you became unhappy about the money side of the deal and suspected that you would have been quietly disposed of once you had done your bit. You were therefore insisting on cash up front, which was not acceptable to Mr Sweet.'

'Well, of course, he would say something like that,' Greening said. He seemed to Michael to be making an effort to sound casual, but he was sweating and it was not only the sheepskin coat to blame.

'I don't know why you should say that,' said Honeypot. 'Incriminating you would hardly buy him any favours.' She waited but Greening, though thinking furiously, had nothing to say. 'There is another point that requires clarification,' she resumed. 'You gave the impression, perhaps unintentionally, that you went abroad as soon as your wife was threatened. We don't know precisely when the threats began but we know when your wife was injured and hospitalized. We also know when you flew abroad, using your spare passport. That was four days later. So there were at least four days not accounted for. Mr Greening, when you come to discuss your position with me you had better be prepared to explain what you were doing during those four days.'

Honeypot explained later that she was

doing no more than fishing for statements that might give her a fresh avenue to explore, at the same time keeping him on the line while others attempted the almost impossible task of locating his mobile signal without even knowing which country he was in. Michael could think of several more or less incontrovertible answers that Greening could have given, ranging from 'preparing to shut up the house' to 'visiting a lady friend', but Michael was not the one under pressure. It also struck him that Honey, whether or not she had seen the danger, might be pushing Greening in the direction of settling somewhere within the EC and supporting himself by means of a series of email frauds directed into Britain over the Internet. Greening was caught off balance by seeing his position, which he had thought impregnable, being undermined.

Honey's voice was speaking again. 'I don't mind telling you this,' she said. 'Springing surprises on the defence often only promotes sympathy in the jury. So I may as well go on. It came to our notice that your wife had been expecting an upturn in your finances. So we have been looking into your financial affairs. You were appointed to your current, well-paid post only recently. Until then, you were broke. When you took up this post you bought your present house. Unfortunately you bought at the top of the market and stuck yourself with a substantial mortgage. If you had waited even a few months, house prices were going to fall; but you didn't know that. So you have what they call negative equity. Yet you have been assuring people, including your wife and your bank manager, that better times were coming. The question you have to answer, Mr Greening, is where were they coming from?'

Michael had been watching the expressions passing over Greening's face like the shadows of clouds on a hillside. Those, plus the man's posture, gave away his reactions as Honey drove wedge after wedge into his confidence. As soon as Greening first said that he wanted to keep his whereabouts from Honeypot, Michael had realized that Hilda and he would be stumbling blocks. Greening must now be regretting his mention of Geneva – unless that had been a bluff. Watching Greening in the light of that realization, he could see a stiffening of the man's spine as he prepared for ruthless action; and as Honeypot uncovered the flaws in Greening's hope of being found innocent, the hope that the man would be satisfied by fading into obscurity wilted and died. Greening was psyching himself up for desperate action. The effort of doing so, while forcing himself to act innocent in voice and aspect, was beginning to show.

Michael's thoughts came into focus. He would only have to shout their whereabouts so that Honey could hear and the man would have nothing to gain by killing them; that would only turn a hard-to-prove conspiracy charge into actual double murder. But would Greening think quickly enough and hold his hand? From the beginning, Michael had been aware of a weighty bulge under Greening's coat; he had also been aware of walking into a trap when he allowed Greening into their room but he had wished passionately for the chance to ask questions. He was only now regretting his curiosity but he could spare little attention for regrets. His worry was that Hilda, thinking along much the same lines, might act precipitately and trigger a bloodbath. There was an uncomfortable feeling in his guts.

'You're going to have some difficulty, convincing the detective inspector,' he said. 'It seems to me that you have three options.'

Greening's eyes narrowed. 'Go on.'

It occurred to Michael that it might be to his advantage if Greening thought him as big a crook as himself. 'One, you could stay out of Britain, where you've been rumbled, but sell the whole package again in every country that has a stock exchange.'

'The codes would all be different.'

'You've sussed them out once, you could do it again.'

Greening thought and then shook his head. 'I've learned a lot, this time around. I'd be facing the same dangers.'

'Two, you could get hold of the one really damaging witness against you, Clive Spicer, and persuade him to change his evidence – perhaps by offering him the whole package.'

'Same objection. And the cops will be holding him or watching him like hawks.'

'Possibly. Three, you could persuade the detective inspector of your innocence, or failing her, the procurator-fiscal or a jury. That would mean discrediting Clive Spicer by bribing, persuading or blackmailing some other crook to swear that Spicer had been bragging, while being held on remand, that he was being paid to incriminate you.'

TWENTY-ONE

Silence fell again. The phone lay on the bed, forgotten by Greening. Michael could only hope that Honeypot would continue to listen, but silently.

'I like your third option,' Greening said suddenly. 'But who would I get?'

Michael had been wondering the same thing but the answer came to him in the nick of time. 'In your shoes I would approach Alec Jenkinson through Paul Penicuik. Offer him the whole package, free and clear, as soon as the heat's off you, less ten per cent for yourself.' The words were calm but the tension was rising until he could hear and smell it.

'I like it,' Greening said. From under the sheepskin coat he produced the self-loading pistol that Michael had been uncomfortably sure was there. 'It will work very well. And I can do it from here, so I can't lose. The problem, from your point of view, is that I could never count on it working as long as you're walking around, alive and talking.' He spoke dispassionately as he raised the pistol.

Michael, in his peripheral vision, had watched Hilda bracing herself for action. Everything seemed to happen in slow-motion. With one ankle undependable, he dared not risk a sudden attack. Death would leave little time for regrets, if only it were too quick for pain. At first he was afraid that Hilda would move too soon. Then his guts seemed to do a downward swoop when he thought that she had left it too late. At last she gathered her courage and pounced, quicker than he would have believed possible. She threw herself onto Greening's back and gripped him in the one killer hold that does not depend on superior strength. Her lesbian PE teacher had taught her well. She had Greening's throat in the crook of her left arm, her left hand in the crook of her right elbow and her right hand behind his neck. Greening, who had either forgotten her presence or discounted her as a mere woman and therefore inactive, was stupefied. Michael, as he had feared, was slowed by his ankle but he was just in time to push the pistol aside before it fired a single shot into the bed. It was not very loud, but he felt the heat of the blast on the palm of his hand and the stink of burned powder filled the air. Then he had the pistol in his own hand and the pain in his ankle was again in the forefront of his mind.

Greening struggled vainly against Hilda for a few seconds and then his arms were hanging limp. 'Don't kill him,' Michael said, and Hilda released her stranglehold. Colour came back to Greening's face as blood returned to his brain and a moment later his eyes opened.

The mobile phone on the bed was quacking anxiously. Michael picked it up with his left hand. Feeling absurdly dramatic, he used his other hand to cover Greening with the pistol. 'Are you still there, Detective Inspector?' he asked.

'I'm here, are you all right?' Honey answered, all on one breath.

'We're both fine and I've got the gun.'

'If I'd known that there were firearms

there I'd have intervened,' she said, 'but I wanted to wait until he'd convicted himself. Thank God you're both all right! Make sure that he doesn't have another firearm.'

'I don't,' Greening said, but he raised his arms for Hilda to pat him down.

Shock was just catching up with Michael. 'So you were in on the plot the whole time,' he said to Greening. 'You were really planning to kill both of us, weren't you?'

Greening smiled grimly. 'No comment,' he said.

Michael raised the pistol, which was becoming heavy in his hand. 'Just give me an excuse,' he said. Into the phone he said, 'Inspector, I suggest that you phone your colleagues here and have them do whatever is appropriate.'

'You're still trying to teach me my job. They're on their way,' said Honeypot. 'If you listen out you'll probably hear the cars.'

TWENTY-TWO

Michael and Hilda decided to see out their uncompleted honeymoon at the same hotel. The hotel management would have preferred to be rid of guests who seemed to be followed by trouble, until the media reports brought a steady trickle of guests and bookings by the curious. Hilda and Michael became celebrities whose company was much sought, but their lips were sealed.

In any case, they would probably not have been allowed to leave Switzerland until the giving of statements was completed. This was accomplished with the aid of an interpreter and a handsome and flirtatious local police officer. Michael, whose sense of security had been only slightly raised by the marriage certificate, was relieved when they were free to go home on the due date. They agreed that the whole episode had come as a relief to a honeymoon that was in danger of becoming a bore. They were not in the habit of filling idle time.

Home was undoubtedly best. Home, however, promised at first to be just as boring as Switzerland. It was a relief to throw themselves back into work and to be reunited with Russet before she could put down roots in her temporary home. Honeypot seemed to be avoiding them. Inspector Dodson, to whom had been delegated the task of taking their statements all over again, whispered that he rather thought that she might be feeling culpable, having delayed alerting the Swiss police in order to give Greening time to commit himself. He also pointed out that the process of extradition could never be hurried, especially if the accused was awaiting trial for another offence in the host country – in this instance, discharging a firearm in a hotel room. It was therefore several years before the last of the trials – Greening's – was finalized. Ironically, he was only fined for the crime in Switzerland and was admonished for conceiving the plot without taking an active part in it but he received a heavy sentence from a British court for the intent to kill Michael and Hilda in the hope of evading justice.

Meanwhile, another interesting development had been the unheralded arrival of Estelle at Spring Cottage. Hilda, like Honeypot, had been feeling guilty – in Hilda's case for taking what she now believed to have been a sledgehammer to crack a nut. Michael, for his part, after seeing the effect that Estelle had had on his Hilda, had no compunction and had thoroughly enjoyed his part in the lesson that had been handed out to her.

When Estelle came to call, Hilda was busy in the kitchen but Michael was in the sitting room and just off the phone. Finding his new sister-in-law on the mat and remembering her habit of repaying insult with violence, his first impulse was to turn and run; but she seemed to have no violent intentions. 'I would like to see Hilda, please,' she said simply. Reassured by the mildness of her manner and her use of the word *please*, he led her into the sitting room and offered her a chair before hurrying to the kitchen.

'She wants to see me?' Hilda said. 'Are you sure?'

'That's what she said. And she said "please".'

Hilda's eyes opened wide. That word had not previously formed part of Estelle's vocabulary. Mentally reviewing her lessons from her school's PE teacher, just in case, she went to join her sister. To her surprise, Estelle jumped up and pecked her on the cheek. Estelle was modestly dressed in a skirt and twinset of similar grey-blue.

'What Michael said in his wedding speech. That was aimed at me, wasn't it? Truth, please.'

Michael decided that he would be better out of the way. This was no place for a man. He took Russet out for a walk.

Hilda was in a quandary. Estelle did not seem to be on the warpath, and if she had a quarrel with anybody it should be with Michael. Moreover, having almost forced Michael into preaching what she could only think of as the sermon it would have gone against the grain to let it go to waste. 'Yes,' she said, 'it was.'

Estelle nodded sadly. There was a tear on

her cheek. 'I thought it must be. The point is, I had been saying how respectable we were as a family and what Michael said only added up to poking fun at that sort of pride. Is that what it was about? I think there had to be something in it because all the guests were laughing their heads off. At me! They all recognized it. All these years, have I really been so proud, so holier-than-thou? Did I preach too much?' Hilda looked away. 'I was afraid so. I was only trying to set a high standard. I'm sorry. I must have been hell to live with. I was furious at the time and it's taken me the whole of the past month and a long talk with Father Joseph to come to terms with the facts. Father Joseph explained that nobody was ever thanked for telling an unpalatable truth, and he should know. Can you forgive me?'

'Yes, of course,' Hilda said.

Estelle smiled shakily through her tears. 'I feel so much better now. But tell me one thing. Who was Aunt Edith based on?'

Hilda almost gaped at her. How could she not have recognized the parable of her own behaviour? That should have been the killer blow, the knife in the ribs. According to

Michael, Aunt Edith had tried to incriminate her sister and her future brother-in-law on a charge of cannibalism. Not quite the same thing as Internet pornography, perhaps, but there had been no Internet in Aunt Edith's day. Hilda pulled herself together and said, 'When we came back from Switzerland, the first time, somebody had entered our house, used the Internet to put some child pornography onto our computer and sent an email to the police to tell them that it was there. Luckily, we could prove that we were still on the way home at the time.'

'Well, I think that's the rottenest trick I ever heard of!' Estelle said indignantly. Hilda was watching her face and to this day is prepared to swear that Estelle's surprise and indignation were genuine, but Michael and Hilda have never been able to agree on an alternative suspect. Michael is adamant that Estelle must have been guilty and he reminds Hilda of how she had spoken of her sister's skill at deception; Hilda sticks to her guns. She worries endlessly about the injustice they had inflicted on Estelle but quite accepts that the end result, converting

Estelle from a pain in the public posterior into quite an acceptable relative to have around, was worth a little rough justice.

TWENTY-THREE

Pol Zuis, aka Paul Sweet, was alone in the big house. His staff had been scared away too effectively to be bribed to return and those of his former henchmen who had not been jailed could smell doom in the air.

He never went down into his basement any more. His modus operandi *had invited retribution from other criminals who he had betrayed to the Law, but he had not expected the invitation to be accepted. He had hidden behind a cloak of anonymity or sometimes the identity of one or other of his minions. This had not endeared him to the minions. Now, however, a gang leader for whose sentence he had been responsible had been freed pending an appeal and Paul had been in receipt of a number of phone calls. Some had promised him a lengthy session in his own torture chamber; others had forecast a betrayal of all his most cherished* secrets to the police. Most had promised both. He knew that Clive Spicer had talked but he had also been left in no doubt that his organization, or what was left of it, had been penetrated by a mole.

The heavily curtained study was brightly lit. He got out of his chair and walked heavily into the dining room. This was lit only by light from a remote street lamp. He waited in the doorway until his eyes had adjusted and then walked to the window. The lights dancing across the water no longer had the power to soothe him. The shrubs that had been planted in the garden at great expense were no longer a comfort and a screen against the world but threw black shadows in which anything could be lurking.

As if in answer to the thought, he was sure that something dark flitted from one shadow to another. He waited. Perhaps it had been an owl or a figment of his own eyestrain. Then it happened again, further away, and he only perceived it in his peripheral vision. His spirit was already too low to fall further but he was more aware of the ominous feeling of imminent disaster. Perhaps it was real, perhaps not, but either the police or a body of vengeful rivals could by now be after him. His mind was made up for him. Rather than hang on, straining his eyes and his nerves, waiting for the axe that might never fall, he would slip away. There was plenty of money in his wallet. He need only stay in a big hotel for a few days and make a cautious return in daylight when the heat was off.

In addition to the main front, back and kitchen doors there was a fourth. It was inconspicuous, being hidden behind a clump of escallonia that had been allowed to spread unchecked. It opened from a small room where once boots and shoes had been cleaned. Without putting on any lights he managed to find his overcoat. The door had not been opened for many months but it had been well oiled and it swung open in silence. He locked it behind him and pushed past the branches. The path to the gate in the side wall of his garden showed up pale under the moon. As he neared the gate he paused. Was he being unnecessarily timid? He was not well read, especially in English, and if he had been a reader it is unlikely that Proverbs would have been his choice of reading matter, but he might well have remembered that 'the wicked flee when no man pursueth'. A rustle in the bushes chased him on his way. The sound was made by a large black cat belonging to his neighbour, but it sounded human to guilty ears.

The side gate opened onto an alley between his house and that of the cat-owning neighbour, who happened to be a well-known judge – the sort of householder, in fact, who would have responded promptly and positively if the police had requested access for the purpose of keeping observation on a suspect. The judge's garden wall appeared as a dark rectangle in the gloom but there seemed to be an irregularity, a moving irregularity, above the top of it, such as might be the head of a watcher. This was the other cat belonging to the judge.

He had intended to turn away from the river and towards the network of secluded streets and spacious gardens, but he looked in that direction and saw two figures against the glow of a street lamp. He turned instead towards the river and hurried his pace because he would be too easily hemmed in if he lingered. If he had looked back he would have seen the two figures close in for a kiss, but he did not look back.

Emerging onto the towpath he turned to his left, towards London, past the foot of his own garden. He had been born in a city himself and his instinct led him towards the centre of town. Further along the towpath, in the middle distance, a car was parked. It held another pair of lovers, but his mind was not on amorous thoughts at that moment. He was coming to another alley, wider than the first. He turned into it, but within a few seconds a car halted at the further end. There was a street lamp nearby and he could make out the police livery and insignia. A figure in a peaked cap got out and entered the mouth of the alley. The constable in the driver's seat had had too many cups of coffee and was looking for a place where he could have a discreet pee, but Pol Zuis was not to know that.

They were closing in on him. He gave some thought to what the future might hold if he were sent to prison and decided that anything else would be preferable – the prisons must hold many men who had lost their liberty and their livelihoods because of his machinations. He looked around desperately for an avenue of escape.

Boats were moored along the margins of the river. There was one no more than a stone's throw from him. It was a neat motor cruiser with a generous cabin. He could lie low there. He was no swimmer but the river was low after a long dry period and much of the space between *him and the boat was bare mud. It looked firm enough to take his weight. His only worry was that his footprints might remain to give away his hiding place. He need not have worried.*

It chanced that his first two steps away from the bank landed on a balk of timber that had been lost from the boatyard upstream and was now lying buried just below the surface of the mud. His third step came down on thin, wet, glutinous mud and he went in up to his crotch. His other foot being held up on the timber, he was thrown forward onto his face. He was stunned by the shock of it for some moments but then he began to struggle. He managed to roll onto his back but by then the mud was chest deep. That was when he should have screamed for help, but he was obsessed by his fear of the police. He stretched down with his feet, hoping to find a hard bottom under the mud. If his legs had been ten feet long the move might have saved him.

When they found him in the morning, only his hands were showing. They were clasped in an attitude of prayer.